A Collection
of Outdoor Tales

Books by Russell M. Cera

Fruit of the Bad Seed
Cry Wolf, Cry

A Collection of Outdoor Tales

Russell M. Cera

Libra Books, Inc.
West Islip, NY 11795

Libra Books, Inc.
West Islip, NY
www.LibraBooks.net

ISBN: 0984825029

PRINTED IN THE UNITED STATES OF AMERICA

Dedication

The stories in this work are posthumously dedicated to Dante Cera and Grenville Lyon, men who have inspired me with their appreciation of nature's bounties. They were most responsible for my love affair with the great outdoors.

Contents

Acknowledgements

Foremost, I would like to thank my cherished friend and confidant, William Rives, for his humor that often makes my day, his wisdom that I truly respect and his word that I never doubt.

Thanks go to my wife Linda for her patience and suggestions that have contributed to the writing of Cry Wolf, Cry. Also, my sons Victor, Gregory and Steven must be acknowledged for backing me in this effort. Their encouragement when reading the initial manuscript draft was my incentive to go forward.

The following people have also inspired the writing of most of these outdoor stories: Jeffrey Lyon, James Carapezza, Rosario Adragna, George Johnnidis and Andy Bocchiaro.

My friend, Grace Z. Protano, author of *As Long As You Can See the Clock*, You're Okay and *Absent from Class* of ProPress Inc. must receive my appreciation for her talented editing of most of these stories.

My nephew, Russell Cera rceracreations.blogspot.com did all of the cover and interior artwork for this anthology.

Introduction

From as far back as I can remember I was drawn to the outside world in any season.

In springtime, a sip of water from a mountainside rill tasted so much better than a drink from the kitchen faucet.

The summer's honeysuckle fragrance and the sweet smell of a freshly cut hayfield had an appeal. The odor of floral wallpaper did not.

In fall, the fruit of bittersweet bursting red, yellow and orange complemented the multicolored vista of autumn's beauty. To be indoors at that time of year was abhorrent

In winter, the silence of forested landscapes wearing the cloak of the season's white intrigued me, and I could not wait to go outside. I wanted mine to be the first footprints in the snow.

At all times, the sight of a rapid stream in a sylvan meadow, or glimpses of wildlife were exciting and I always wanted to be in that realm.

Many times I have been asked to clarify what motivates my desire to hunt and fish. Most questions came from anti-hunters, gun control activists, or simply from people who could not comprehend what I found so alluring about nature.

Recently, however, I received a letter from a fellow wolf enthusiast asking the perpetual question. Because we shared a common interest, and I wanted her to realize how I could be both a conservationist and a huntsman, I wrote the following reply:

I recall many times being asked: *"Why do you hunt?"* Answers short of a thesis seemed too abstract and never sufficed or were comprehensible, so I've seldom attempted to rationalize my desires. It was like trying to simplify something as complex as the emotion of love, or trying to interpret my definition of a thrill. Who could ever explain the goodness of Santa Claus or the spirit of Christmas to a child?

But I respect the question for there seems duplicity in a man to love animals, want to preserve them, yet would prey on some. In my view I see less insincerity in *attempting* to harvest from nature what I would eat, and more hypocrisy in those who would raise animals for slaughter and condemn the manner in which I take others.

All I offer in defense of my attitude toward hunting and fishing is that I realize I am an omnivore, like **all** mankind, the **ultimate predator.** As Man, we take from Earth far more than any other animal, and yield **nothing** in return.

I realize I do not have to hunt to survive; but as in every predator on the planet, I believe I am driven by an atavistic urge to seek and chase my quarry.

I grew up in a rural part of New Jersey, the son of

Italian immigrants. When my father first came to this country in the early 1900's, he hunted and fished as a supplemental provider for his family's subsistence. Every adult I knew, hunted and fished. When I heard the stories my father and his companions told of their outdoor ventures, I could not contain the enthusiasm to become part of those tales.

Any game bird, rabbit, squirrel or deer that was hunted was done so for consumption. My Dad and those old-time hunters never killed an animal for "fun." I have followed that tradition, never hunting for an animal that I would not eat.

Difficult to understand, and perhaps more problematical to explain, is that I take no pleasure in the kill. As an angler, I can catch fish for pleasure, and release those I do not intend to eat. This is not possible for the huntsman, and leaves me with ambivalence for those few times I am successful. It is not the killing I enjoy, it is more the chase.

As far as the huntsman's role with respect to conservation, most people don't know that the **Pittman-Robertson Wildlife Restoration Act,** passed in 1937 has raised billions of dollars from taxes on hunting licenses and related equipment for wildlife preservation and the protection of natural resources and wildlife habitat.

In 2009, a record of nearly $336 million was raised by hunting and related activities. The same kind of tax applies to anglers under the Dingell-Johnson Act; rods, reels, lures and other equipment provide funds for game and fish departments. There are absolutely NO other conservation causes that contribute as much to wildlife.

I do hope that my love for field and stream does not interfere with your perception of my love for wildlife.

* * *

Do we reject that modern day pursuits may be attributed in part to the survival benefits they provided for our prehistoric relatives? Studies show we are drawn to vistas, perhaps because of our ancestors' behavior of surveying the landscape to avoid danger or view hunting opportunities. Similarly we are drawn to the sight and sound of running water; it is clean and potable.

Being the biological organism he is, I suppose there is some logic to the huntsman's assertion that he is helpless to follow instincts encoded in his DNA. Yet I will offer no such logic, but will not deny my connection to the natural world. I only know that I am blessed to have lived my life with an innate desire to hunt, fish and gather.

The thrust of these stories is not to explain the outdoorsman's role nor justify his sport, but rather to convey what the bounties of nature have offered those of us who appreciate her heritage and have experienced the inexplicable exhilaration and thrills afforded by the magnificent outdoors.

My outdoor adventures have taught me tolerance and appreciation. Without them I would not have learned respect for another man's passions, nor would I appreciate the other gifts given to me in my lifetime. These infatuations have engendered more love for my family, have made me value my friends and have given my life a positive purpose without need to seek gratification from less noble directions.

Some of the stories in this collection are products of my imagination while others are true accounts of my experiences afield. All were written to reflect reverence for the natural world and the creatures therein.

Those who share delights similar to mine will be indulged in these tales, but my hope is that the anthology may also illustrate to others the enchantment to be found in the fields, streams and woodlands of our outdoor legacy.

Rufus and Rastus

I'm not sure how old I was, but I was too young to attend school when my father bought two beagle hounds he named Rufus and Rastus. From the very beginning I liked Rufus. His name was easier for me to say and no matter how I tried when the pups first arrived I'd say: "Rufus and Rassiss."

My mother would sing the lyrics of a zany tune to make me learn the pronunciation. "Rufus Rastus Johnson Brown. Oh watcha gonna do when the rent comes round?"

It took practice, but when I finally got the names right, I could not have imagined how attached I would become to both dogs. Nor could I have foreseen the impact of joy and sorrow those two pups would have on me when I first saw them.

I was sure an artist painted their coats. Finger-like oceans of brown fur separated contrasts of black and white islands into a seascape of color. Both puppies were so much alike, though different enough to distinguish one from the other.

When they drank, their ears drooped long and thin well beyond their noses, and I'd fret as the velvety lobes dipped into their water bowls. I'd pick up the pups to dry their ears and laugh as they nipped at my fingers and bit their ear-tips instead.

My father built the best coop and run any dog could have. The pen was secure enough to keep the hounds in, but not efficient enough to keep me out. I could never leave the pups alone and I'd get scolded nearly every day.

"Figlio mio," My grandmother would shout. "Pleasa. No go in-a doga house."

I'd come out of the dog run when she called, but the next day I'd sneak into the pen again. I loved the pups' soft, wet licking of my face and neck and I liked cuddling them both until they fell asleep in my arms.

I played with Rufus and Rastus all through the summer. They were my best companions; they were my only companions; they were the catalysts for my love affair with dogs.

* * *

One November evening while my mother was giving me a bath, I heard my father's repeated shouting for the dogs.

"Mommy, why is Daddy calling Rufus and Rastus?"

"He went out to feed them," she told me.

Usually when my father went to their pen I'd hear them yipping and barking their excitement. When I didn't, I became afraid.

"Did they get loose?"

My mother shook her head. "Maybe Daddy just let them out for a run."

I could barely stand still long enough for her to towel my hair dry and make me put my pajamas on. Barefoot, I slipped and nearly tumbled down the stairs. I ran into the kitchen where my father stood clutching the dog bowls to his chest. The expression on his face was as difficult to see, as it was to answer his question. "Russell, did you unlock the dog pen today?"

I knew I had, but I couldn't answer.

"They're gone. Rufus and Rastus are gone," he said.

It was the worst news I'd ever heard. I began to cry, and I recall that night as being one of the longest of my young life. Sleep would not muffle my hearing as I listened for their barks. Fatigue could not stop repeated trips to my bedroom window as I looked through the darkness at an empty dog pen.

For several days my father drove around looking for the dogs. One time he let me go with him. As we rode through the neighborhood and drove along wooded areas I'd try calling through the open car window, but my voice would get stuck in my throat and I found it easier just to cry. It was the last time we searched for my two best friends.

* * *

Days that seemed more like weeks passed and I began to dread the oncoming winter. "If it snows what will happen to the dogs?" I asked my mother.

Not even she was able to console. "Mousy, maybe they'll come home before it snows. It's not your fault that they ran away."

Even my father tried to comfort me. "Russ, I think someone stole them, or they'd have come back by now."

Then, a few days later, early one morning my grandmother had gone out to get our milk delivery and found Rastus licking at the cone of cream that had risen up through the neck of a frozen milk bottle.

I hugged Rastus so hard it must have been difficult for him to breathe, and I kept looking over his shoulder expecting Rufus to appear. My father kneeled down to pet Rastus and saw the dog's paw pads worn from black to pink, and that his neck was nearly rubbed raw.

"Look, Russ," my father said smoothing the hair under the dog's neck, "the person who stole him had him tied up."

He may have said it to make me feel better, but I still had the sting of guilt hurting inside my chest. "Do you think Rufus will come back?" I asked.

He shook his head without answering. Rufus never came home.

* * *

The frigid cold of winter made me beg my parents to allow Rastus to live in our house. It was against my father's wishes. Dad felt that a hound should be kept outdoors if it was to become a hunting dog, but he gave up on training him. I think my father was as sad as I about the loss of Rufus, so he let Rastus be my family pet rather than train him to go afield.

Spring arrived and with it came a stronger attachment to Rastus. Though at first I felt a closer connection to Rufus - if only because I could pronounce his name - I adored Rastus.

It was in early May, on a day that songbirds and daffodils beckoned us outdoors. I was wrestling with Rastus in our front yard when two ladies walking a dog on the other side of Michigan Avenue distracted him.

I have nightmares of the scene. As he bolted across the busy thoroughfare I can still hear the sickening thud. The speeding, black car never braked or swerved in attempt to avoid killing Rastus.

It was the first time I encountered death. For a boy who was not old enough to attend school it was an experience he should not have had to suffer. That incident cut short a love affair between a dog and me. It left me convinced I'd be oblivious to any hurt I would ever know, but I could not have been more wrong.

Of Vanishing Birds, Dogs and Neckties

When I was a boy I learned to love hunting. I suspect, however, that my affinity with it came even before. I fantasized about it and lived in its omnipresence. As I grew older, the sport was changing, and I had a recurring, bad dream. I constantly harbored the fear that one day it would be no more; that one day I would go afield to hunt and I would search and search to try to find the birds that were no longer there.

* * *

A while ago I ultimately gave in to my German shorthair's incessantly nudging muzzle and pleading eyes and took him for a run. It was against my better judgment, for he is far too old. His back quarters are painfully gripped by arthritis and his vision is weak, but the heartaches he gives me to take him hunting are far less bearable than my having to nurse his aching joints and sore muscles afterwards.

For several days I had endured his pleas, waiting for inclement weather to subside. As soon as it did I grabbed his belled collar, and he, in his heart at least, was an ecstatic pup again.

He was in the habit of gathering toys as some dogs will, but the most unique idiosyncrasy was with a belled collar. I'd trained him with it and put it on him only when he hunted. It was used so that I would know where he was in heavy brush, but mostly, I confess, it was for me. Whenever I would hear their dancing jingle stop, my heart would quicken in anticipation of a point.

For him, though, it meant hunting. Whenever I was home during the cooler seasons he would take it off its hook and there sit, ears perked and amber eyes fixed on my every move with that collar draped from his jowls. An accidental bump of those bells in any season was my misfortune, and I'd pay dearly for it.

Due to his age I was reluctant to put him in rough terrain. Remembering a spot not so distant from my home where I had actually trained him as a pup, I decided to give it a try. It was the place where he had made his first point.

Passing by there once I noticed that developers had done some clearing, but I did not know to what extent. I had seen some bulldozers and dump trucks stalking there, perched like raptors as if to do their evil, but I gave those machines only a desultory thought. It appeared there still remained acreage enough for birds to survive and for a dog to run.

My heart sank as we arrived. I knew immediately that my estimation of how much land clearing had been done was wrong. I felt sad for my dog. Although some game could remain in those isolated patches of cover still standing, he'd be hard pressed to hunt it. Ghastly gray, cement foundations loomed in acreage that was once a sylvan scene.

It was at one time immense fields of wispy grasses and milkweed interspersed with tangles of honeysuckle, patches of blackberry and Queen Anne's lace, colored by dashes of bittersweet and splashes of goldenrod. Then, bobwhite and pheasant reigned, not workmen. Now, contractors rule and those unfortunate birds are the exception trying to survive on meager fringes where slight bands of cover refuge those stalwart few.

How difficult it is to see this place now. Once quail were counted by the covey. Pheasant would flush in bevies and the number of points the dog made in a day was too numerous to recall. But that was too many years ago. Now, where the whir of wings and the raucous squawk of the cock pheasant once unsettled the composure, the drone of engines shatters one's nerves. The din of man had arrived. I should have gone. I would have gone, but his whimpering got to me and I let him run.

As I watch the old dog try feebly to find those familiar scents, I'm sad again, and again I reminisce. My mind wonders to years when I was a youth. Those memories, though fond and treasured, are rarely explored. They make me sad to know they are of delights forever irretrievable to me. More sadly, those memories are of joys, times and places my sons and their sons will never know.

* * *

I daydreamed of a huntsman – a gentleman huntsman in a necktie. The spirit of youth, the hunt, the child dwelling in me now was that hero to the boy of me then. He was my father and he kindled in me the hunting fever I thought would never subside. He was the very essence of the sport I love so much and so much loved to share with my dog. That huntsman was the cupid responsible for my romance with the enchanting outdoors.

I grew up in a rural area of north central New Jersey where deer, small game and birds -especially the birds-abounded. Becoming of age to go afield myself only cast in stone what my father had molded by his example and tales. As I explore the imagery of my recollect, I can see that old, stained, corduroy, hunting jacket he wore. I've never seen a corduroy hunting-coat before or after, but I'll never forget it. Nor can I ever forget the tie. He wore a necktie to go hunting. He was a magnificent huntsman in a necktie. No one wears a necktie to go hunting, but he, I thought, was in vogue. It fit the image: a gentleman huntsman who dressed in deference to his sport.

The respect he held for the hunt was manifest in his youth when it supplied the table of an immigrant family and was, at times, its total subsistence. Naturally, in my mother's house, the hunter need not sustain the family; my dad the railroad engineer did that. Nonetheless, reality seldom distorted my childhood perceptions and I supposed him to be the hunting provider, the grandest huntsman whose larder never was unfilled.

How exciting those stories were that he told, how intriguing they were to me who yearned to go along on the hunt. Of course, being too young to go, I was kept at home. Nothing, however, could keep my imagination at home, and so it flew.

Whenever he was off hunting, I, too, was afield, and I the provider. I was at times the heroic Indian brave returned to a hungry camp with my trappings. I was the successful pilgrim welcomed to the village with needed game. I suppose, philosophically, every hunter feels there is something atavistic in his wont, an innate drive spawned by his predatory ancestors. As it was with me, I imagined it no other way. The boy, the child, the spirit in me now was that hero to me then and so I learned to love the sport that way.

He is gone now. Those days and times are gone now. Gone, too, is that old, brown, brush-worn corduroy coat; and I never see a huntsman in a necktie any more.

Oh, how I wish for that return. How I wish I could look once more at those decrepit, sepia photos of him and his hunting friends displaying abundant game. As a boy I would look at those pictures over and over, fascinated by the proud, unsmiling, gentlemen hunters, the birds, and the neckties. Carelessness has lost those photos, and so even they are gone now.

Where he hunted and taught me to hunt is changed now. I am changed now, too, but that spirit of the hunt exists and no one could have made more a demigod of the huntsman in the necktie.

* * *

Somewhere within my daydreaming and the watching of that aged, German dog, my melancholy gave way to lightheartedness. I became glad for my dog and content to know he had lived the life he had during that particular time. What times they were! Then he had done what he most loved to do — hunt. His every thought during his wakeful time was dedicated to it, and, I suspect, even his dreams were occupied therein.

Together we were out at every chance. I remember his first whimpering efforts to tag along. I recall clearly that first awkward point, and can vividly see its contrast to the classic ones he made later, perhaps his last, I fear.

As I watch that unstinting shorthair labor along, my thoughts drifted back to those years we teamed up to hunt those game-filled fields. It was during that time that the pastoral scene began to change so drastically. As I stood and saw him check to see if I were near, I recalled how difficult the last few seasons were. Once the bucolic landscape was a haven glorious for him and me. Now it is changed.

A few years ago it began. As if a giant land rush was on, soybean, corn and rye fields vanished. Builder's stakes were everywhere. The foreboding, excavation markers ominously portended the condominium cities to come. New homes and shopping malls sprung up so fast that the land is now transformed, unable to be hunted.

The heartbreak of watching my dog search those game-barren places where I must now go has convinced me. Having an animal with the inbred desire to hunt and nowhere to do so is abhorrent to me. And so it is that I'll be content in what we've had in those innumerable hours afield, countless hunts and myriad birds. They afford me my dearest memories and his most fulfilled part of life.

As I looked for the dog I realized that these times and places can never be again. They are lost forever. And so as I strained against the extraneous noises of civilization to hear if the waltz of the bells had stopped, I made a decision

I never dreamed I'd make. It seemed so remote from my every pleasure, but necessary to preserve those perceptions we all must keep. Now I knew I did not want to hunt any more. At least not hunt for birds and certainly not without that great German dog. I don't want to walk another field without him.

From beneath my necktie, within my thickened throat, that tear-barring lump that arises on such occasions came a shaky call: "Atta boy Spark, go get 'em old guy. Go get 'em."

I knew full well that my urging would only serve to make him try harder. The last thing he needed was to exert more effort on those staggering casts. But, what the hell, he was having fun and had I not tended him as I always have, he may have thought I was disappointed in his work. I could not stand that, so I'd make the tremulous call again, and again he'd course and check the wind to try to find the birds that were no longer there.

Of Promises and Posted Signs

"Dad, this land is posted," the boy announced with obvious disappointment as we arrived at the spot I had promised to take him.

"I see that, son. We'll go somewhere else," I weekly reassured.

What had just happened gouged emptiness within me. Not because the land was posted, but because I had just lied to my boy. There was no "somewhere else" to go. I had made a promise to take him small game hunting on that first day of the season and I hated to disappoint him. This, after knowing of his sleepless nights in anticipation, was unsettling to me.

As we drove away, one glance across the driver's seat was all that was necessary to stir that dreadful choking in my throat. The boy was looking out the window, searching hopefully for ground without poster signs. It was unbearable to see that confidence, so prevalent in youthful eyes, diminish as the miles went by.

Not so long ago I vowed to give up small game hunting and stayed with that pledge for several years. I did this quite easily after the loss of my dog; it was only for him that I continued to bird hunt in those last few years he was with me.

The obligation I felt to take the German shorthair hunting was now replaced by another, more demanding charge. My 11-year old son has caught the hunting fever as I had hoped he would and begs to go afield. Now I am faced with a difficulty more abhorrent than any I have known with respect to the hunting and fishing I've done over the years. How do I make him understand the differences a generation has wrought?

How do I tell a youngster that those things I so loved to do when I was his age are forbidden to him? How do I defend something so natural as going afield against the growing antagonism toward it? Pushing those inevitabilities to the back of my mind I raced with precious daylight to win his favor. I thought that there must have been some open land around where I could take the boy for an hour or two to pay the debt my promise owed.

As I drove along searching for the hunting fields I once frequented, I offered only reminiscence to the boy. There was no consolation for him as I told him of the pheasant and quail that once abounded where now asphalt parking lots and condominiums loom.

Later I pulled off along a railroad track and parked the car. The boy's face lit up and I was thankful for the meager brush-line along both sides of the railroad bed. It brought back memories of a pointing dog, a huntsman in a necktie and another excited youth.

For the moment I could see myself tagging along behind my father as he hunted along railroads many years before. He was an engineer for the Jersey Central railroad and always felt comfortable being on railroad property. Besides, game was abundant there. Rabbits would set in the dense underbrush and pheasant would congregate to peck cinders needed for their crops.

Most important for me, though, was the excitement dancing in the boy's eyes and the fact that there were no poster signs. Fifty feet on both sides of the tracks is railroad property, and would never be posted.

For the moment my reveries are real. I am excited. The stage is set and I am going to watch the play unfold. For this performance the birds and dogs with their predetermined roles are the players, and the huntsman is the protagonist. The land is the backdrop, the setting for the drama I so believe in. Once I had the lead, but now I am content to observe. My son's debut is about to be played and I am his enthusiastic audience.

No sooner had we gotten our gear from the car, we encountered a lady walking her dog. When she realized what we were about to do, she stormed in a torrent of screams. The anti-hunting epithets she spewed were not new to me, but the boy was dashed by the abusive tirade.

I was ambivalent about explaining to the woman that we were within our rights to hunt along the tracks. I like to show my son a respect for the wishes of other people, even though most do not share what I believe the land and the game animals are there for.

I also know too well the belittling feeling of being chased, and wished the boy not to experience that shame. To spare the indignity, I told him to get back into the car and as we drove away I noticed tears welling up in his eyes and only hoped he did not notice mine.

We drove through the countryside. As we did, I could not help thinking about the encounter. Most people are blind as to the hunter's role in the natural scheme of a wild heritage. Deer, birds and other game species thrive because of the hunter, not despite him. Game as that woman would have had it would be like beasts in a zoo. How sad it is that a zoo may be the only place for children of future generations to know of such animals.

Every back road and farm lane I reacquainted myself with held more disappointment. The little guy just sat quietly next to me seeming to sense my hurting inside. It was then that I thought of a farm not too far away where I used to get permission to hunt. I had given up hunting the farm when I learned that the farmer's sons, whom I had often taken afield, grew up and moved off to make their livelihoods in other businesses.

For my sake, I hadn't returned because I knew of plans to sell portions of the land and did not want to see what developers would do. Besides, when the farming stopped, I knew the birds would become scarce. For my boy's sake, I drove in that direction nonetheless.

I suppose the apprehension I held about knocking at a door I hadn't entered for so long was not as strong as my curiosity. The farmer and his wife who had owned the land were old, and I wasn't sure they'd even remember who I was, but I went anyway.

As we reached what remained of the fields once used for corn and soybean, I was shocked. The farm was gone; the land divided. Houses stood in places where my dog once stood fast on point. Intuitively I felt that it would be wrong to go to the old farmhouse, so with the boy at my side I knocked on the door of the newest home.

The woman who answered the door was not receptive. I could tell she was annoyed at our presence. When

I asked about the old farmers, she was blunt about their having passed away, and with equal chill quickly changed the subject to how much she disliked hunting. When her husband joined her at the door he, too, lectured about how the hunters shot up all their birds and that now they had none around for their kids to see.

I guess my son was listening, but I could not make my attention suffer the ignorance. I kept thinking of how often I had hunted with the farmer's sons and how they too once looked at and appreciated the birds. I wanted to tell them that it was because of the old-time hunters that pheasant were there to begin with, but I held back. I offered our apologies for having disturbed them and I left with more evidence of the growing disdain and the boy with yet more disappointment.

It is not the lack of courtesy or even the contempt these people have toward the hunter that I lament; it's the lack of understanding. The hunter, as I know him, is conscientious about environmental conservation, a final vestige of a heritage once beautiful. The huntsman represents those yesteryears when a man could go afield and teach his sons the appreciation of wild things, open spaces and a love of nature.

He is not to blame for the demise of the game, or the devastation of the land on which it lives. The culprit dwells within the omen of the poster sign. When there no longer is acreage to hunt, game and many others animals will perish. The laws written years ago by our hunting forefathers protect game and other species. The statutes provide funding from the hunters' to ensure it. Take away hunting, our wild heritage will surely follow.

Oh, how I have often wished I could freeze the clock that melts off the little time left for the native birds, the stream born trout and the wild deer, but here I'm dreaming again.

As we again drove the roads I had traveled years ago, I felt a guilt that made it difficult for me to speak to my son. It was past lunchtime at that point, so I offered to stop and get a bite to eat, but he refused. He, as I, had no appetite. I was sure he did not want to stop for fear of losing time. He clung to the hope that I would still take him hunting. Perhaps I should have taken him to the state land. However plastic that seemed with its designated areas and planted birds. For all I regarded it, I could not bring myself to go there.

Game animals should be free, and those who pursue them, unrestricted. What I know of wild birds, pointing dogs and huntsmen of an era passed is what I wish for my son. It is, though, an evanescent wish and I should learn to let it go. But for the boy I cannot.

So I turn my car and search the roads and try not to notice that the pacing sun is now lower in the November sky reminding me that little time is left to keep my promise to the boy.

I press the accelerator and clench the wheel. The boy, still paused at the edge of his seat, wide and liquid eyes hopefully fixed on every passing post, announces like a knell in a tremulous voice, "All the land is posted, dad, – all the land."

Of Hang-ups, Hats, Bugs, and Big Deer

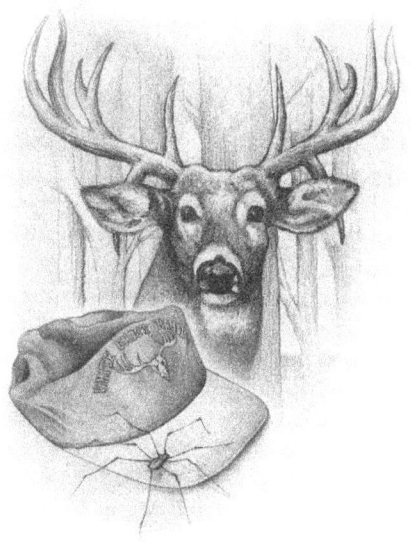

Deer hunting is a solitary sport, but I don't like doing it alone. I like company. Not only on the journey to and from the deer camp, but in the woods as well. The camaraderie at the lodge dining room is a favorite time, but for me it's not enough. If I had my druthers, I'd like company all of the time. I'd even appreciate a buddy in my deer blind. Seems strange, but that's me.

One season the silly obsession turned my Texas trip into one of the most memorable hunting adventures ever. I have a few friends who love to hunt, but not as many as I'd like. Those with whom I do go hunting aren't into guided hunts. Perhaps they don't like to pay the price. I'm retired, living on a fixed income and social security, but I save my dimes to go to Texas once in a while.

Because of my obsession for companionship, without the luxury of companions, I invited Ralph. From the beginning I had a premonition that my invitation was ill conceived. I met Ralph and all of his idiosyncrasies on a hunt in Alabama several years ago. He's not a bad guy. In fact, his enthusiasm is quite infectious and he's fun to be around sometimes, but he's walking paranoia. He has more hang-ups than a clothesline and strung out tighter than one holding a week's worth of wash. But I like company.

I'm the kind of a guy who'll let a stranger take a swig of my beer, eat whatever is served and will sleep in a lean-to, as long as I can go hunting. But, heck, that's me. Ralphie is completely different. He won't put his mouth on anything that's not sterilized, eats only the food he brings with him wherever he goes, and won't sleep anyplace that doesn't have accommodations like the Hilton. This makes him a difficult traveling companion, but he loves to go hunting and that's why I like him.

One of Ralph's hang-ups is bugs. It's probably the only one I can actually relate to because I've been bitten by ticks, chiggers and mosquitoes, stung by wasps, hornets and bees, but none of these has ever kept me out of the woods.

Ralph will not go anywhere in the vicinity of these creatures unless he has taped his wrists to his gloves and his ankles to his sox. I've seen him do it.

Inviting Ralph to Texas had as much to do with where I hunt as it did with my penchant for playmates. I have been a guest at the White Ghost Ranch in Doss, Texas, which is as close to five-star as anyone will ever get. The only insect I've ever met there was a housefly and he was out by the barn and appeared lonely.

Ralph, I knew, would love White Ghost, as long as he brought his own food and plenty of masking tape. I told him over and over that neither was necessary for where we were headed, but he packed it all anyway.

I believe our trip says more about my hang-ups than his, because I was a wreck, not Ralph. I wanted things to be perfect. No bugs, immaculate accommodations and plenty of big bucks for my man to see.

At the White Ghost, the odds were in my favor. I couldn't miss, but as soon as we were picked up in San Antonio, I began to fret. As we piled into the pickup truck Ralph's first question to the guide was: "Are there any snakes in Texas?"

It occurred to me that a question to a Pennsylvania miner about the presence of coal in Newcastle might be as redundant, and I knew immediately that the Texan's honesty was not going to serve well. "We have a few rattlers, but they should be denned up this time o' year."

The answer got Ralph's attention. "Rattlesnakes? What do you mean '*should be*' denned up?"

"Well, when it's hot like this, y'all never know, but not to worry about our place. I killed only two this entire summer, and they were little 'uns."

A Texan's definition of "little" would even get my attention, especially if he were talking about snakes, but Ralph immediately lifted his feet off the floorboard and glanced over his shoulder into the bed of the pickup. "I don't like snakes," he said. It was his only understatement of the entire trip.

"Ever get bit by one?" asked Ralph.

"Twice, but my boots saved me some. I even got bit by a brown recluse once, and that was a lot worse than a rattler."

"Brown recluse? What in the name of hell is that?" Ralph shouted.

"Li'l' ol' spider. Got a pretty mean bite though."

All of a sudden I began to sweat from the fire of Ralph's glare. I consoled myself by thinking he'd see the biggest deer of his life. I figured he wasn't going to see a snake, but I wasn't that sure about spiders, so I changed the subject. "How's the deer heard this season? Many big guys running around?"

"Well, they're there, but with this heat, I don't know how much runnin' 'round they'll be doing."

"That's news," I said as I tried to avoid Ralph's stare.

The ride to the ranch was tedious. Ralph had his feet up on the dashboard, and I had my eyes glued on the Hill Country terrain, hoping to spot just one of the hundreds of deer I bragged we'd see in Texas. No matter how much I prayed, not one revealed itself on that tedious ride. It was 85 degrees and I could swear it was getting warmer.

When we got to the ranch, I felt a little better with Ralph's approval of the lodge. "This is top of the line," he said as he inspected the label of the cellophane-wrapped muffins and cakes graciously put out for us.

"What are you looking for?" I asked.

"The expiration date."

"Just squeeze the damned thing. If it fights back, don't eat it!"

Thank goodness the goodies were fresh. The only thing I needed after he squeezed the moisture out of every muffin, crumb cake, honey-donut and candy bar, was for the deer to show up when he went on his first hunt. I love that ranch and I knew I was going to have a good time, but I wanted him to have a better time.

I don't know why I can't learn to keep my mouth shut, but I'm weak and can't help myself. "Ralphie my boy," I said with my most encouraging tone, "now, when you go out later, don't shoot the first buck you see. You're going to be here for four days and you'll keep seeing bigger and better bucks."

I was speaking from experience. "The big guys usually aren't the first ones to show up. Yearlings, does and immature bucks come out first, then, the shooters will show up. The five and six year-olds come later."

I knew so much about deer, I was certain I impressed Ralph. In fact he told me so when he came back from his initial hunt, having seen the biggest buck of his life, — the very first deer to show up at his blind. I could sense myself morphing into an idiot.

Mood swings are another of Ralph's little quirks. He was sky high when he told me about the buck. "I never saw such a monster! I wanted to shoot that deer so bad I could hardly sit still, but your words kept ringing in my ears. 'Don't shoot the first buck you see,' so I didn't."

He looked directly into my eyes as his mood dropped to a low and said: "He never came back. I saw a lot of bucks, but he was the biggest."

I didn't know what to say. He was distraught. My big mouth was responsible, but it did manage to impart a few more words of deer wisdom that I would later regret. "When those big guys do come in, they usually don't stay long. At this time of year they're looking for does. Once they leave they don't come back."

Later at dinner, after he rewashed his clean eating utensils and made the cook double-scrub the lettuce for his salad, Ralph slowly began to come around. "I can't wait for tomorrow morning. Man, am I excited! But don't worry, I won't shoot the first buck I see."

I didn't know what to make of that last remark, but I thought it best to keep my trap shut. I thought I sensed some chilly vibes from the ranch's owner. I'm not so sure he thought much of my expert deer advice.

The next morning was cooler and the deer moved a little better. I saw some nice bucks; I even let a few shooters walk. I found myself more interested for Ralph and how he was doing. I was resigned not to take my buck until after he got his deer. The last thing I wanted was for him to get skunked and for me to get a nice deer.

When we returned to camp that morning, I felt a sense of relief to find Ralph on cloud nine. There he was with a good buck, snapping pictures, shouting with joy and yahooing like the giddiest kid in the Texas. "He's not like that one I saw last night, but he did show up first."

"Well I'm glad you didn't follow my advice," I said. "You got yourself a beauty."

"But I did follow your advice. He showed up first and I let him go. A few minutes later, here he comes again, and again I let him walk away. But when he came back again a half hour later, I figured it was an omen. You said, 'once they leave they don't come back,' so I shot him."

A tremor ran up my spine and stiffened the hair at the nape of my neck like when I'm caught in a lie. Ralph's buck was a nice deer with good mass and high tines. It was the biggest deer he had ever shot, but it was not the trophy I knew he saw on his first hunt.

I was thinking he should have waited, because I knew he'd see better bucks, but my guilt wouldn't let me say so. The guy was listening to my brilliant deer expertise and acted accordingly. My motor mouth had done it again, but Ralph seemed happy and I was glad for that. I hated those down moods of his and didn't like being responsible.

The next morning, I took my buck, a 250-pound, high tined 10-point with a 21-inch spread and good mass. Another mistake. When I got back to camp with that deer, Ralph's mood plummeted to rock bottom. I guess he realized that he should have waited for a better deer than the one he got.

I dreaded what I had in store for the remainder of the trip. My only hope for his mood to swing upward again was his decision to hunt for another buck.

When I take a deer I'm delighted. It's always a thrill, but there's a twinge of ambivalence. It's hard to explain, but whatever I'm feeling, it will not allow me to celebrate. Ralph, on the other hand, becomes effusive. I've never known anyone to get more excited.

When Ralph shot his second deer, a 164 B&C with a 24-inch inside spread, he was ecstatic. But I outdid him. I was hooting and hollering so loudly, folks thought I had gone mad. But those people did not experience one of Ralph's downers. I was never so happy for anyone to take a larger buck than mine.

On the White Ghost Ranch, picture taking is a biggie. As Ralph posed with his buck, the rancher switched Ralph's hat for one with the ranch logo. Thinking that it was a new cap, Ralph's grin would have shamed the Cheshire cat and his pictures showed it. After the photo session, I saw him examine the hat for a second or two and discover it was not brand new.

Paranoia came to the surface. Ralph fretted about having worn a cap that some other person had on his head. Ten minutes under that hat was too much time for Ralphie's head. While our host was with another hunter, Ralph finally got the sympathy of a ranch-hand to switch the hat for a brand new one. He was happy again.

A few hours passed and the picture taking resumed for another hunter's deer. The photo shoot was being rushed a bit because of the heat. Perspiration poured from everyone, especially the hunter who was straining to hold his pose with a heavy deer.

Ralph was the only one who seemed cool. Except for when he nearly kicked a hole through the wall of a shooting box to stomp a daddy-long-legs to death, he was as calm as I'd ever seen him. He was all-smiles, enjoying life. He had killed the biggest deer of the party and was proudly sporting an untainted hat.

After a pose or two, the photographer realized that the lucky hunter did not have a White Ghost cap. He called a guide to fetch one, but he held up in mid-sentence when he bumped into Ralph beaming over his shoulder.

Sometimes things seem to happen in slow motion. This was one of those times. Everything was in still-frame as the photographer saw what he wanted perched atop Ralph's head: a sparkling new cap. To save time, he snatched the hat off Ralph and slapped it on the stranger's sweaty head. Ralph was not happy.

"Did you see that?" he whispered to me.

The look on Ralph's face would not have been more ghastly had he seen a rattlesnake or a brown recluse. I tried an answer. "See what?"

"My hat! He put my hat on another person."

I knew I was not going to pacify. "It was only for a second."

After the pictures were taken, Ralph's hat was handed back to him. I don't know if anyone noticed, but he took the bill of the cap between his thumb and index finger as if he were pinching a cockroach. I felt a little sorry for him, he really liked that new cap, and I knew he'd never wear it again.

"Listen, pal," I said. "I'll swap you. You can have mine. I only wore it for the pictures and I wasn't even sweating. Honest!"

Ralph finally calmed down after we traded caps. I was flattered that he accepted the swap. Although he's probably never worn it, I'm confident he'll keep it as a souvenir of the best hunting trip of his life. It was a favorite of mine. I truly did like his company, but hey, that's me.

Cry Wolf, Cry

It was daybreak and Lakota set out to hunt alone, a choice fraught with peril for even the most able of hunting wolves.

When he caught the odor, Lakota hesitated. The gray wolf was puzzled. The smell of venison that he had been following mingled ominously with the noxious smell of man, and Lakota glanced around.

The wolves of his pack had not eaten in a week, yet they remained behind. Hunger gnawed at their stomachs, but unlike Lakota, they refused to hunt without Bartok, their leader. Bartok was preoccupied. His mate was in labor and he and his pack would not let her stay alone.

Lakota, too, was reluctant to leave, but another drive spurred him to venture. He knew his presence at the den site was not as necessary as bringing food to the alpha female. She needed strength to give birth, and nurture her pups.

The deer Lakota was searching for would feed the entire pack if he could locate it. The carcass was covered with three inches of spring snowfall, but Lakota's keen nose led him closer. When the wolf caught the smell of man mingling with the deer meat, he shuddered to a stop. Experience told him to abandon the dead deer that now lay a few feet away. Another instinct urged him on. For him, the survival of the pack depended upon his decision. Lakota ignored his fears and dug with his forefeet into the snow.

An excruciating pain shot up Lakota's front legs as the spiked jaws of the spring-trap crushed shut on his paws. His scream reverberated off canyon walls, echoed down into the valleys, and carried through the great pine forests back to the wolf pack.

At the den, Bartok jerked up his head. The entire pack heard Lakota's screaming, but only Bartok would respond.

When Lakota realized he was caught, he yanked backwards and the trap moved with him until the attached, three-foot chain reached the end of its slack. When it did, the wolf flipped over and twisted violently, cracking the bones in his forelimbs. The injured wolf realized that he was at war for his life and must fight it the only way he knew how. He clamped his jaws onto the cold steel with such force that he snapped one of his canine teeth, and badly chipped the other.

Again he cried out, and again he bit down on the relentless hold of the insidious trap. Lakota's agony grew worse as he struggled for freedom, twisting and jerking against the scourge. He sat back on his haunches and stared at the metal menace stabbing spasms of pain into his forelegs. Lakota looked over his shoulder desperately hoping against the improbable that his brother Bartok might appear.

Slowly he extended his tongue to lick his throbbing paws. The soft, wet tongue gave no relief to Lakota's pain, so he dragged it over the ice-cold steel offering peace to the tormenting trap. Feverishly he licked at the jaws, hoping they might loosen, but he managed only to wash away the loathsome scent of man.

Moments passed in agony and again the lone wolf glanced toward his home. He thought of Bartok and wanted to howl a call to his brother. There was little hope that Bartok would come to his rescue, but Lakota kept glancing in that direction nonetheless.

The pain in Lakota's legs turned from piercing spasms to searing heat, its fire consuming the nerves throughout the front of the wolf's body. The animal lifted its trapped legs to peer at the iron contraption, and wondered what kind of enemy this jawed monster was that held him in its deathly grip. When he did, Lakota realized he could no longer feel his front extremities. Panic overcame him and he shrieked a woeful wail to call for his brother.

Bartok heard it all. To leave his mate in the throes of labor was abhorrent to his very fiber, but to ignore the cries of his brother, struck a chord even more deeply embedded into the loyalty of his lupine nature. His brother was in need, and his lifelong mate dependent. With overwhelming ambivalence he made a decision.

Barreling through drift after drift, Bartok sprayed snow into the icy air. His muscular chest and powerful strides defied the frozen, white powder and he rapidly crossed the expanse between him and his brother.

Shivering in the snow, Lakota knew nothing of the reality that lay ahead. If he did, it would not have been fear of dying that made him quake; it would have been the fear of living without his front feet. Had he been caught in the trap by a single paw, he could survive by gnawing through the bone to free his leg and make his way home. Life would be difficult, but with Bartok to help him, he might survive.

Having both front paws locked in steel jaws, high on his shins, Lakota was doomed. No matter how attentive Bartok would have been, a two-legged wolf would be a burden to the pack, jeopardizing its survival.

Lakota's only thoughts were of escape, and his only alternative was to chew through his paws. Before starting the gruesome task, Lakota glanced over his shoulder. He saw something! For better vantage he forced himself up on his haunches into a position that resembled begging.

Snow swirled up on the horizon. Something was forging through the blear straight toward Lakota. Through a mist of hot breath and exploding white powder came a bounding, black dot two hundred yards away. It became bigger and bigger as it neared. At a hundred yards, the dot grew into a figure, and nearer, the figure grew into a wolf!

Bartok, at full stride, was fifty yards away when Lakota recognized him. Lakota was saved, if only in his mind.

Before his brother could close the final distance, Lakota squealed a delighted yelp and rolled onto his back, momentarily forgetting his plight. When Bartok got to him, Lakota shook his entire body in an attempt to wag his tail. Bartok licked at his brother's muzzle.

Lakota never took his eyes from his brother expecting Bartok would solve his dilemma. Bartok poked his nose at the trap and pawed at the chain, following it to a ring that was spiked into a huge tamarack stump. Realizing that the ring could not be loosened by a pull, the wolf sniffed at the wood to which it was attached and began to gnaw. Pausing only to rest his aching jaws, Bartok was an hour into his chore when he heard the noise. In the distance, he recognized the drone of the snowmobile.

The two wolves cowered in the snow hoping the sound would not come closer, but it did. Lakota had no choice, but Bartok could escape the frightening figure that now climbed from the strange machine and trudged toward them.

The buckskin clad boy stared at the cowering animals. It was the first time the wolves had ever heard a human voice: "Looks like lobos need help."

The young descendent of the Nez Perce stepped closer for a better look. Bartok snarled and made a mock charge and the boy backed up a few paces. "Ho, now. Didn't mean this to happen."

Both wolves watched as the youth retreated backwards until Bartok stopped growling. Then, the Indian turned, jogged to his vehicle and sped off.

* * *

When Bartok calmed enough to resume gnawing at the wood, he had only gotten an inch deeper, when the man-machine returned. Now, two people carrying rifles approached the wolves. Menace snarled from Bartok's growl; Lakota sidled closer to his brother. Again, Bartok stood his ground in front of Lakota as one man took aim.

A shot rang out. Bartok yelped. He growled at his attackers, but would not retaliate. Lakota could only whimper and nuzzle against his brother.

As moments passed, Bartok became unsteady. Then, a second shot was fired, hitting Lakota in a flank. The wolf tried to turn to bite at the dart protruding from its hip, but the trap and chain prevented it. Bartok swung around to comfort his yelping brother, lost his balance and fell forward. He tried to get to his feet, wobbled and fell again. Several minutes had elapsed before both wolves succumbed, eyes open, but asleep.

* * *

It was late in the day before Bartok began to stir. His body twitched as he tried to push himself up. Within a few minutes he was able to gain his equilibrium; within five more he was steady and on his feet, and the first thing he did was to look for his brother.

Bartok whimpered when he realized Lakota was gone. The trap and chain were also gone; the heavy scent of man was all that remained. Bartok tried to track his brother's spoor, but the only tracks in the snow leading to those of the snowmobile, were human.

By the time Bartok gave up his search, darkness had fallen and the snow reflected a ghostly yellow from a lunar glow. Bartok lifted his head to the moon and heaved a baleful bay that lingered in the icy air before rising to bounce off the full moon and echo back to earth. To Bartok it sounded failure. To his pack, miles away, it rang sadly in their ears, and they answered.

After a final look around, Bartok set out for home, his posture sagging, his gait desultory. When he arrived, the pack, his mate and four new pups met him. Though the pack's greetings would help lift his spirits, he would forever mourn the loss of his brother. Hardly a night would pass without Bartok calling to his lost kin with a howl that held a more sorrowful tone since Lakota's disappearance. In a distance, only malevolent wolves heard the call.

* * *

As he drove home from the meeting, Jeffrey Reese was transfixed with the snowflakes dancing in the beams of his headlights. Reese considered the men who had been so vehement about wolves, and he thought about his dog Gretchen, and spoke to the snowflakes pelting the windshield.

"How can so many people disdain the wolf and yet love their dogs? I just don't see that much difference between the two."

Despite the disconsolation he felt after the Farm Bureau rally, Reese was glad to be home. At the door, Gretchen could hardly contain herself, squealing and shaking her whole body to flag her greeting.

"How's my girl? Miss me, did ya?" Reese laughed. "C'mon Gretch, let's take a walk before we hit the sack."

Reese spent the next half hour playing with Gretchen in the fresh snow. He was tired and wanted to go to bed, but he couldn't disappoint the dog. He knew she looked forward to her nightly jaunt and he forced himself to please her.

The next morning, Reese nursed a steaming cup of black coffee as he arranged his notes. The German shepherd curled at his feet had been his only companion while he worked on his assignment.

Reaching down, Reese rubbed the back of the dog's ears. Gretchen rolled her eyes back and nudged her nose toward his face when the phone rang.

"Hello."

"Hello, my name's Joe Morton. Is this Jeff Reese?"

"Yes, it is."

"Charley Wittington, the conservation guy? Well, he told me you might be interested in something I got."

"Yeah, I know Charley. What do you have?"

"A gray wolf."

"A wolf? Is it alive? Where is it?"

"Yeah, he's hurt pretty bad, but Doctor Ferris says he thinks he can fix 'im up."

"Are you sure it's a wolf?"

"Oh, it's a wolf awright. An Indian kid caught him in a trap. Says he was trying to catch a wolverine or something, and caught the wolf by mistake."

"Where is it now?"

"Right now he's over at Doc Ferris's place. Wittington says you're writin' stories 'bout wolves and you might be able to help me. I been livin' in Montana my whole life and never seen a wolf before."

"I'm a journalist doing a series on wolves in the Bitterroot area. How can I help you?"

"Charley says you might be able to keep the wolf a few weeks until it heals up enough to let it go."

"Well, that'd be an experience. You sure Charlie said it would be okay?"

"Yeah. He says that your place is kinda far away from town, so no one will know you have him."

"Is he crated?"

"Biggest cage we could find. Wittington says his guys will build a fence for it if you agree."

"Well, then. Sure. Bring him over."

Turning to his dog, Reese hung up the phone. "Did you hear that Gretch? We're going to have a relative of yours staying with us for a while. C'mon, let's go for a walk and we'll talk about it."

Gretchen barked, spun around and wagged her tail as Reese put on his parka.

* * *

The next evening when Reese looked into the cage, his heart sank. Crammed far back in a ghastly cage cowered a pitiful creature. A large cone collar around its neck and soft-casts on both of its forefeet; the animal whimpered its plight.

"Except for his teeth, he looks worse than he is," said Charley Wittington. "His legs are fractured and the trap cut him up some, but otherwise he'll be good as new in a month or so."

Reese was wondering if he did the right thing in agreeing to keep the wolf. "What'll I feed him?"

"Raw meat, road kill, anything it will eat in the wild. But don't worry about that. I'll bring you all you need."

Reese turned to Morton. "You said something about another wolf being with this one. Was it hurt, too?"

"No. He seemed okay, but really mad. He was trying to chew the trap off a log to free this one here. Almost got it off, too."

"It's a good thing he didn't," said Charley. "This guy would have died with that trap hanging on him. Between him and the pack, they'd a chewed it away, paws 'n' all."

Reese shook his head. "What a horrible thought. I don't even want to think about it."

But the wolf was the only thing he could think about for the next week as a crew from the forest service built a huge holding pen.

Lakota was trapped again, and the smell of man was everywhere. Whenever a human would come near, Lakota's terror gripped tightly, squeezing the muscles of his bladder until it lost control. It was painful for him to walk, so he stayed on his belly, far back in the cage. He tried to bite at the bindings that held his legs, but the collar would not allow it.

When the enclosure was completed, the wolf was brought in and the restraining-cage opened. As soon as the men were far enough away from the cage, Lakota burst through its opening into a faltering run. When he reached the fence of the enclosure, he realized yet another obstacle between him and the life to which he so desperately wanted to return. Several feeble dashes along the pen's perimeter weakened the wolf and it collapsed in exhaustion as far from the restraining-cage as it could get.

For the next few days Lakota circled the enclosure searching for a way out. Finally, the defeated wolf began to give up his life, refusing to eat. This had Reese worried.

Reese noticed that the wolf's coat had lost its sheen. He thought its sagging hindquarters were signs of starvation. The wolf seemed to cling tentatively to life by drinking water, the only human offering it would accept.

Gretchen would often go to the enclosure to inspect the stranger. When she neared the fence, the wolf would approach her. Slowly, as if trying to satisfy a curiosity, Lakota would stretch his neck to nose the wire. With its first sniff, it appeared to Reese that the wolf recognized a familiarity.

Whenever she was near, Lakota would limp close to Gretchen, sniff through the fence, and lay down nearby. This unexpected behavior of the two canines gave Reese an idea.

"Gretchen, I think you can get him to eat. What do you think?"

Reese spoke as the dog wagged its tail. "If you understood what I had in mind, perhaps you wouldn't be so exuberant, young lady."

Jeff grabbed a sack of fresh deer meat, leashed Gretchen and brought her to the enclosure, and tethered her inside. He stroked Gretchen's head. "Sit! Stay," he commanded. The obedient dog sat immediately and Reese looked to the far corner of the enclosure. There, penetrating wolf eyes were fixed on his every move.

Glancing at the wolf, Reese was hoping his plan would work. The thing he counted on the most, however, was Gretchen's gender.

Reese talked to Gretchen as be backed away, as though trying to convince himself rather than the dog. "Male canines rarely hurt females, despite the species."

With the dog inside the pen, the wolf could inspect this creature with a tolerable odor. As Lakota drew near, Gretchen dropped to her elbows and yipped. With the attitude of play in her body language and the signal of friendship in her wagging tail, Lakota slowly came closer, his tail tucked beneath him. The wolf's neck fur was bottle-brushy, its ears pushed back and its nose extended.

As their muzzles met, Gretchen came out of her crouch and the two distant cousins, stiffly but slowly, inspected each other. In slow motion, Lakota's tail emerged from between his legs and stiffened out behind him. Almost imperceptibly it moved and then slowly waved its canid hello.

Moments lingered as the dog and the wolf tested scents both new and ancient. The dog was playful with its lively step, the wolf more guarded with a stiffened stance, but between them, a peace was evident.

Then, Gretchen did what Reese had hoped; she became interested in the meat and ate several pieces. Seeing this, the wolf crept nearer. Lowering his body, the wolf inched forward and sniffed at the pile, straining to get closer without taking a step. Stretching his neck as far as it could reach, he snatched at the nearest piece and swiftly dragged it beyond the length of Gretchen's tether.

Four times the wolf came back for hunks of meat. The dog tried to follow, but its leash held it back just as Reese had planned. Finally, after weeks of severe hunger, Lakota had eaten.

* * *

For several days, Reese fed the wolf this way. Soon, Reese would no longer tether Gretchen when he put her into the enclosure. Not only had his dog earned Lakota's confidence, Reese too, was able to gain acceptance into the enclosure.

Gretchen's fawning actions toward Reese seemed unacceptable to Lakota. To understand what the dog found appealing in the human, the wolf sniffed at Gretchen wherever Reese had touched. It took days to accept the man with guarded trust, and another week before Lakota allowed Reese within reach.

Three days later, Wittington phoned. "Hello, Jeff, Charley here. How you doing?"

"Hey, Charley, I'm good. You?"

"Good. Good. Listen. The reason I called was to see if you needed more meat. But also, Doc says it's time to remove the casts off your wolf. We'll have to dart him, so I'll bring everything."

Charley heard a laugh in Jeff's voice. "Bring meat. It's all we'll need."

"What do you mean?"

Reese paused, playing with Wittington. "You don't need to dart him."

"Why not?"

"Because it's off already."

"The collar fell off?"

"Everything's off. Collar, casts, everything."

"How did that happen?"

Reese took a deep breath. He knew his answer would confuse. "I took the collar off last week, and he unwrapped his own legs."

There was silence before Wittington said anything. "You removed the wolf's collar without darting him?"

"Yeah. I figured he suffered enough without traumatizing him more."

Wittington was still confused. "A wild wolf allowed you to touch it? I know his teeth are shot, but he can still rip you up with what he's got. How'd you do it?"

"Gretchen helped me. I've been able to approach him for days now."

"I don't believe it. I've heard of people who've raised wolf cubs, but I've never heard of anyone taming a wild one."

"No. I wouldn't say he's tame. And I don't think anyone else can touch him without Gretchen being there."

"Well, whatever. But don't get too attached. You know we're going to have to release him."

"No problem. I hate seeing him in that cage."

The following weekend, Wittington, Doctor Ferris and two men from the Department of Conservation came to get the wolf and return it to the wild.

"How do you guys plan to do this," asked Reese.

"Well, unless you know a better way," Whittington said, "we're gonna have to dart him. How else can we get him in the crate?"

Turning to Ferris, Reese asked a question as though he expected a negative reply. "Doc, do we have to shoot a dart into him, or can we just give him a shot by hand?"

Looking into the enclosure, Ferris tilted his head down to peer over his reading glasses making it obvious that he noticed the wolf was down on its belly as far away from the men as it could get. "Yes, we can, but by the looks of it, I don't think he's going to allow that. Do you?"

Reese saw Whittington shake his head, but would not be discouraged. "Charley, I think I can give him the shot."

Whittington slowly took a toothpick from behind his ear, clamped it in his teeth, raised his brow and looked at Ferris with a shrug. "Your call, Doc," he said, the toothpick barely moving.

The doctor glanced around at the other men before speaking to Reese. "I guess it's up to you. Giving the injection is easy," he said as he fixed his attention on Whittington.

Whittington shrugged again, removed the toothpick and continued the slow shake of his head. "No problem by me," he said retuning the toothpick to his mouth. "Besides, I gotta see this."

Reese broke into a wide grin. "If you guys stay out of sight, Gretchen and I will take care of it."

After a brief lesson on administering a needle, Doctor Ferris, Whittington and the other men got out of sight. Reese called

Gretchen and entered the pen. As soon as they were inside, Gretchen made a dash for the wolf, and it rose to meet her. Reese slowly approached as the dog and the wolf made their usual greeting: the dog, a sniffing Jell-O mold, shimmering with delight, the wolf, a gelid form, suspiciously sniffing back.

From several feet away Reese could see the wolf was not as calm as it usually became when it played with Gretchen. Shivering, it kept scanning the fence-line and glancing at Reese while trying to accept Gretchen's playful overtures. When Reese saw the wolf become more interested in Gretchen, he dropped to his knees and crawled slowly to get closer, extending his hand first toward the dog, then gently toward the wolf.

After nearly fifteen minutes, Reese could see the wolf was no longer trembling, and he was able to put a hand on its shoulder. Though Reese was shaking more than he anticipated, within a few more minutes he was able to calm his hand long enough to slip the needle into the wolf's fur. Reese was totally surprised he didn't get bitten.

Allowing Gretchen to stay with the wolf, Reese carefully backed away. When he emerged from the enclosure the men waited for him to walk far enough from the pen before they came out of hiding.

Doc Ferris extended his hand. "Congratulations. I'm impressed. You should have been a veterinarian, Jeff. We could use one in the area."

Reese handed Ferris the syringe before shaking his hand. "That wasn't as easy as I thought it would be."

With his hands in his back pockets, Whittington stood wagging his head. "I can't believe what I saw. I thought for sure you'd get bit."

"Want to know something Charley? So did I," said Reese looking into Whittington's eyes.

Ferris turned to Whittington. "I think wolves fear us above all other animals, don't you?"

"When it comes to man, there's something about the wolf I can't quite understand," Whittington said looking past the enclosure into the vast evergreen forest as if the distant wilderness held an answer. "The damned animal will fight a boar grizzly to the death to defend pups, yet an entire pack will run off if a single man raids its den."

"Not surprising," said Ferris.

Whittington shifted his gaze from Ferris to the tree line and again spoke to the forest. "Heck, I've talked with trappers who've approached a wolf in a leg trap. They tell of holding a hundred-pound male down with a stick, yet they say it takes two men with steel nerves and bludgeons to subdue a twenty-pound lynx."

Reese listened to the illogical truth. "I don't know. Maybe it's not fear as much as it is — respect. Seems to me that wolves hold man to a different standard than they do the other animals."

"I wish I knew," said Whittington. "But I guess you're right. It seems to go beyond fear. It's as if they seem to know and consider our superiority."

"I do know this," Ferris said. "Except for the apes, compared to other animals wolves demonstrate more emotions and are far more intelligent. They're a lot like we are. I suppose that's why they've allowed us to domesticate them into dogs."

As soon as the shot took effect, three men lifted the wolf into the crate and onto a pickup truck. Wittington looked at Reese, but could not catch his eye. "Jeff, we're going to pick up the boy who trapped this guy so we can return him to where he was caught. Do you wanna come along?"

"No. You go on ahead. I'll hang out here and see to Gretchen. She needs a little attention."

"Yeah. She sure got upset, didn't she? I thought she'd have a fit when we handled the wolf."

"She'll be okay," Reese said looking toward the cabin where he had locked the dog while the men were crating the wolf.

"I'm sure she'll be fine, but will you?" Doc Ferris asked with a laugh.

Reese smiled. Wittington gave his thanks and Lakota was on his way back to where his traumatic ordeal began.

* * *

When Lakota awoke he fell as he tried to get up. After a few moments he stumbled dizzily to his feet, lost his balance and fell again. The wolf lay still, sniffing the air and glancing around. Lakota felt thirsty and dizzy, but something else began to filter through cobwebs of confusion; something about his surroundings was eerily familiar. Slowly his head cleared and he began to realize his whereabouts.

The feel of freedom streamed through Lakota like a current of joy, while a shock of fright bolted from his memory of this awful area. He scrambled to his feet and wobbled awkwardly, but swiftly, away from the hellish place.

The wolf managed an unsteady gait until it was far enough away before stopping at a small stream to drink. The taste of the icy water sprung memories of dens, familiar wolves and brothers. Lakota thought of Bartok, and it righted his bearings. After a rest, Lakota became more balanced and stronger as he trotted north, following instincts, following scents and familiar trails. He was finally going home.

Lingering soreness prevented Lakota from traveling rapidly, but his progress was steady and direct. The wolf, nearly halfway home, caught a scent and turned his head to peer over his shoulder. The scent was that of a lone wolf and Lakota bristled.

Old wars and territorial battles crossed his mind as he rechecked the odor. The wolf that left the marker was not from Lakota's pack. He was certain he was in his old territory, Bartok's territory, but the marker suggested otherwise. Lakota knew no wolf would cross into Bartok's domain. If it did so by accident, it would not leave a marker. Lakota also knew that the wolf that left it would fight to the death to maintain it. The marker told Lakota to keep out.

Still, Lakota pushed forward. He had to find another sign that might indicate why a strange wolf had trespassed into his old bailiwick. He ambled on with a pace tempered by a more cautious step.

Soon, Lakota found what he had feared. As he slinked to the top of a flinty formation he gained a vantage point from which he could survey a portion of the Bitterroot Valley, his old home. There he trusted his nose for an explanation.

The morning updrafts told the story. A new pack of wolves had moved in, and as suddenly as he had felt the exuberance of freedom, he knew the despair of disappointment. He was among wolves again, but he was alone.

To be within the territory of a strange pack was certain trouble, and he knew he must get out before being detected. Lakota turned away and plodded back toward the boundary he had crossed. When he reached the scent marker he stopped, glanced backwards, then urinated on the spot, a final defiance before moving off.

A party of three wolves from the strange pack was on the prowl. They were searching for a wolf. They had discovered the marker left by Lakota and were eager to punish the interloper. The wolves broke into a trot and headed for their enemy. With the wind in their favor, the trio was able to get to within thirty yards of Lakota before he heard them.

As soon as he saw the marauders, Lakota lowered his head and slid to his belly trying to appeal to their mercy. The malevolent three growled viciously, bared their teeth and snarled. Despite Lakota's submissive gestures, he knew immediately these wolves would not accept him, but it was too late. He had allowed killers to get too close. Lakota was surrounded, and he bellowed, long and loud, ringing soulfully to distant hills.

* * *

It was early in the day when the cry rang out. Bartok sprang to his feet and snarled at yipping pups to quiet them. He cocked his head to listen for what he thought was a distress call.

Restless to resume their play, the pups again began to yip, romping with each other, tumbling and squealing loudly. Again, Bartok scolded the pups until his mate escorted them away. There was something about the yowl that made Bartok decide to leave and he trotted away in the direction of the call.

Lakota was surrounded. Three wolves growled violence as he cowered against a tamarack stump. There was no way he could defend himself. He looked at the malicious wolves and did not have to wonder what kind of enemy these jawed monsters were that cornered him. He looked at the enemy as death, growling and snarling, just as he had looked at the deadly spring-trap that nearly killed him.

With enraged wolves threatening his life, Lakota wailed again. Then, all he could do was to put his back to the stump and prolong the attack by snarling back. Lakota's size made the wolves hesitate. Minutes passed as a standoff continued between the four wolves until the attackers became aware that Lakota's teeth held little threat. Death inched its way closer to the hapless wolf. Lakota glanced desperately beyond the killers. He saw something!

Powdered dirt billowed on the horizon. Something was streaking from behind the three menacing wolves on a direct line toward Lakota. In a cloud of breath and rolling dust came a charging, black speck, growing larger and larger as it closed. Closer, the speck grew into a form, and closer, the form grew into a wolf! Bartok, at top speed, was only yards away when Lakota recognized him.

At full blast, Bartok slammed into the largest of the three antagonists, sending it sprawling and running for its life. Turning to the other wolves, Bartok focused his anger on the remaining duo, and charged.

Fur, fang and fury collided as Lakota flung into the fray, snarling and snapping into a whirling mass of stabbing, slashing teeth, biting, ripping and tearing. Bartok would not need his brother's help in the fight, but Lakota's loyalty would make short work of the melee and ensure victory. Within seconds, the war was over. The beaten wolves scattered and fled, yelping their defeat.

Bartok nuzzled Lakota, inspecting for wounds and found only scratches. Lakota soothed cuts on Bartok's shoulder. Confident that neither was badly hurt, the brothers licked sloppily at each other, squealing and yipping like puppies, rolling over and sidling up to each other. Both wolves were so vigorous in showing their jubilance that they exhausted themselves to demonstrate it.

After a short rest, the brothers trotted homeward. Bartok led the way without looking back. It was Lakota that paused as he crested a knoll and stopped. He took a final look behind at a place he would never forget, nor to which he would ever return. Then, the magnificent gray wolf swung into a run to catch up with his brother.

Despite the sophistication of his body language and the multiple meanings of his vocalizations, Lakota could not tell the wolves of his pack where he had been or how he was able to return. Bartok and the pack would never know that man was responsible. What mattered to Bartok and his wolves was that Lakota was back. Though Lakota had broken teeth, his legs would become sound again, and all that mattered to him was that he was back. Once again, the wolves were reunited and that was all that mattered to any of them.

The Great Brown of the Millrace Pool

The large pool was quiet, deep and dark. From above the pool, the black water courted transformation; it lightened as it squeezed through the millrace sluice, tumbled brighter over the dam and turned to milk as it crashed to engage the rocky bottom. Here it frothed to white foam before marrying into the darkness of the giant pool. Near the pool's shallow tail beneath a willow overhang, a pair of spawning catfish darted about each other. They were unaware of the menace slowly rising from the depths behind them, the great brown of the Millrace Pool.

The trout was unusual, a sable tan. Innumerable dime-sized, orange spots each with an areola of black, painted the fish's flanks. Other spots of gold, crimson and amber diminished in size towards the tail and upper body, reducing to dots, then specks of darker hues that finally shaded into the blackness of its ebony back. The trout's uniqueness, though, was not its color, but its size.

As the trout rose, it veered left near the surface. Its great breadth swirled even the swifter water cascading into the Millrace Pool through a sluice in the dam of the ancient gristmill above. The fish made the whirl with jaws agape, surging the cooler water through its gills, absorbing the oxygen of the more turbulent flow. The fish's course took it towards the tail of the stream's deepest pool. Several yards ahead frolicked the small catfish that would be doomed.

The maws of the enormous trout snapped shut! Its needle teeth ahead of the force sliced through the back and underbelly of a hapless prey, the male catfish. The attack was swift and unsuspected. It came from behind and above and its savagery was deadly. The little fish's life was over, but at the instant of impact, an emission of milt issued from the victim and dispersed into the churned waters.

The power of the great fish had pushed the water past an ovulating catfish. Panicked by the event, she darted away, skirted the bank and thrust herself beneath the soft mud only a few feet away from where the big, brown trout had sounded.

The pool was silent again, save for the rumble of water tumbling into it from the backwaters above the spillway. The great brown, hunger unabated, undulated its three-foot form to surge forward and upward to again stalk the shallows of its domain. The big fish carried out its rounds as ritualistically as it had for the past eight years it had been in the Millrace Pool. The pool was his and he surveyed it with an impunity dictated by his bulk, massive head and sinister hooked jaw.

As it slid through the placid shallows where moments before it had killed the catfish, the mammoth brown swam over the whiskered head of his victim and ignored it. The great fish fanned its tail to push itself to the left and again toward the depths of the black pool. The thrust once more disturbed the water. It swirled up silt and carried it with traces of milt to join a cluster of eggs in a turbid mixture. On that April night, the union initiated life.

The gestation period of mud-catfish eggs varies. In late May, with the conditions as they were in the Millrace Pool, the eggs, miraculously fertilized weeks before, began to hatch. Each ovum pulsated into life beneath the ooze of the river bottom, emerged as tiny fry and by early September grew into adult, mud catfish.

The great brown shared his waters with a few trout above five pounds, several smaller rainbows and a few brook trout. None of these ever took a lie in the center of the pool. For their awareness of the big fish, these trout stayed at the very head, the far tail or the more shallow sides of the hole. Two big browns and one seven-pound rainbow took positions in direct alignment with the gigantic fish – but reverently, several yards behind.

Occasionally, a large fish would have the temerity to take up the coveted spot, but these intruders were transient, only there for a short time, and only in the absence of the great brown trout. Upon his return he did not have to chase these interlopers; merely sidling abreast of these fish sufficed. They would seek more comfortable waters. This was not necessary for the pool's local denizens; each knew the great fish and witnessed the fate of those not heeding his sovereignty.

* * *

Whenever a large trout was caught and displayed as a trophy, excitement would travel among the fishermen who frequented the beautiful park. One trout, the seven-pound rainbow was taken on a nymph in early June. The fly fisherman who caught it spent seventy years dedicated to his sport. It possessed his waking hours and became a tryst for his dreaming. His was a total commitment to the craft. Though it takes as much luck as it does skill to catch such a fish, few are taken by men of less resolve.

The grizzled fisherman caught the big rainbow using his favorite ruse, two wet flies tied in tandem; the first of which fooled a small brook trout. The hooked brook trout was writhing for freedom in the rush of the millrace spillway when the seven-pound rainbow rushed toward the struggling little brookie. Like a catapult, the rainbow made a lunge for the trailing wet fly. The ferocity of its strike thrust the hook deeply into the grizzle of the trout's lower jaw, and it held.

The weight of the larger trout gave resistance to the smaller fish and the brook trout broke free as the more fragile tippet separated. Had the old fisherman known that the bigger rainbow was hooked to the fly on the heavier leader, he could have made the fish spend itself sooner. Instead he had to allow the crafty fish its tenacity and time to sulk at the pool's edge, lessen its fatigue, and fight afresh.

It was during one of these respites that it happened. The great brown of the millrace swam up to and lingered near the hooked rainbow. This afforded the trembling man a look at the two fish side by side. The seven-pound rainbow was dwarfed by the enormous brown of the Millrace Pool.

The weathered angler had caught trout as large as the rainbow, but he always released them. He recognized that fish so large were old and tested, and he felt they deserved whatever time was left to them. He was well known among the regulars who fished the Connetquot. His repute, however, was for never having caught a trout of substantial size.

"Hey old man. Watchya got in yer creel? Six inchers?" boys teased.

"Three," came the reply in a voice warped by age. "Brook trout. Good eatin', though."

The men who knew him were more kind, but not much. "Pop, catch a big one today?"

"Nice size rainbow," he stuttered, "Go well over six pounds, I'd say."

"Turn 'im loose again ol' timer?"

The octogenarian thought about telling of the greater fish he saw, but he recognized disbelief and simply nodded his head.

"Sure you did old man," came a skeptical remark as they'd watch his smile fade to a misty gaze.

After that day the old man fished the pool frequently, not because he thought he could catch the great fish, but because he hoped he might see the majestic trout one more time.

Of those few he told of the colossal trout he saw, none truly believed him. He was saddened to know that others thought him less than forthright, but he, too, began to doubt the incredible fish, so he kept the vigil nearly every day. For the rest of the summer he did not see the great brown, nor did he forget it. Unbeknown that he would one day encounter the tremendous fish again, the feeble old-timer thought of the trout as an apparition and dismissed any notion of catching it. The possibility was remote, and he knew it.

* * *

One of the first mud-catfish fry to hatch nearly became a meal for a swift brook trout. The fingerling escaped when it dived beneath the muck near the bank from where it had hatched. The impending treachery of the great brown had many of the smaller, quicker trout dwelling in the shallows where the baby catfish were. Less fortunate hatchlings became meals. For this, the young catfish population was decimated until only a few remained. These were nearly three inches long, while their frightened brother beneath the mud was nearly one inch larger because of his brazen attempts to seek food in a very hazardous place.

The bold catfish spent little time hiding and it emerged from the mud with negligible heed for that which sent it scurrying. Watchful, it scooted away. It hurried past current changes, tarried near shadows, a protective habit. It darted nearer the bottom and along a sunken bough. Its journey had a destination. Finally, the catfish reached it, a very sheltered place where it could watch for food and not fear attack. It was the only spot in the huge pool where the fish could grow to its fullest potential in the shortest time due to the availability of food and the small expenditure of energy necessary to grasp it.

This shadowed place beneath a vast shroud was where it would always go. It was its secret feeding place, the choicest lane in the entire stream. It was a station that no other fish in the river dared use, except one, its principal owner and landlord, the master fish of the millrace, the great brown! The catfish dared dwell beneath the belly of the behemoth.

As the summer lengthened, so did the daylight hours. The darkness that the big brown loved was less abundant and the fish became more lethargic as the waters warmed. This caused the other inhabitants of the pool to be less cautious, but they still became uneasy whenever the big brown trout wandered. The catfish, too, would become uneasy. Its concern was not for the presence of the big brown, but for its absence. The nearness of the big brown trout protected the little one. Except to occasionally take in more oxygen in the faster water, the great brown rarely left his station in daylight. So the catfish was seldom without his shelter. Nighttime was different. The monster trout prowled regularly then, so after sundown, the catfish had to secure itself elsewhere. The middle of a pool filled with hungry trout was no place for even the most circumspect little fish.

The catfish depended on the brown. Not that the catfish gave much thought to the link, but it knew that whenever the big shadow drifted off, enemies drifted near. This was not comfortable, so the tiny catfish developed a strategy to avoid it. As the days grew longer, the young fish followed close beneath the big trout wherever it went. The great brown was not unaware of his little follower, but was loath to expend the energy to chase it. The big fish tolerated the small one for the five months since they were together; now that the fall approached, they were inseparable. The big fish tolerated this too, – but less.

* * *

When a trout gets to be the size of the great brown, it is instinctively smart. It becomes totally nocturnal and nearly impossible to catch. It rarely miscalculates. Feeding exclusively at night it is less vulnerable to the most expert of anglers. The more weight a fish has, the more the angler's rod, reel, line and skill are taxed until the fish's size becomes an indomitable obstacle. The advantages all go to the fish, frustrations to the fisherman.

Big fish in the Connetquot River have another insurmountable advantage. The park in which they live closes at darkness. Unless something odd happens to alter the circumstances, big trout will live longer and become bigger, turning the cycle again and again, rendering the fish safer and safer to live out their lives unchallenged.

Once, however, an oddity did intervene. The great brown was foul-hooked, snagged by a fisherman's lure. While casting across the current, a novice angler using a large Gray Ghost streamer mended his line upstream. The oversized fly sank deeper into the pool, bumping along the bottom on the opposite side of the great brown trout.

As the fisherman retrieved his line, the leader crossed over the trout's head and the sharp hook inadvertently lodged into the brown's gill plate. The sting of the hook shocked the fish, and its recoil of fourteen-pound fury snapped the leader abruptly! The great fish was free, but not unaffected by the ordeal that would ultimately threaten its life.

Two days had passed, followed by a driving October rain, when the old man returned to the Millrace Pool. He had not seen the huge fish since that fateful day months earlier, but he never lost the hope that he might sight the trout again before the season closed. He thought his dream to catch the fish would never be realized, nevertheless he would try each time he visited the intriguing pool.

Alone, he approached the stream. Quietly, slowly, with the patience of age, he slipped his frail frame down the bank and into the chill of his beloved river. He painstakingly edged his way as stealthily as he could to the tail of his favored pool. There he could cast upstream for the advantage of presenting his flies to the fish and the great brown he knew was there. The old-timer could not resist challenging the overwhelming odds. He had once seen the fish. He knew the fish. It beckoned him. He obeyed.

At the bottom of the pool, positioned close to the large trout, the little mud catfish was more restive than ever; its discomfort warranted. Several times that day the great brown turned and swiped at the small catfish. The great fish had become more irascible of late, and its nasty disposition nearly brought an end to the catfish. The big trout had taken to charging anything of significant size. The cause was the infuriating Gray Ghost stuck in his gill-plate leaving the monster fish in a belligerent mood.

Every fish in the pool was afraid. The titan's temperament had ignited an innate fear. Before, it had been more predictable. It would rise, charge, kill and settle again. Some of his charges were random and inconsistent, but there were also hours of peace from the sated predator, especially during the day.

Now, however, it attacked incessantly. It charged at every sighting of another fish. It chased the larger fish and terrorized the smaller. The menacing brown was constantly in motion and this did not bode well for his pool mates, the little catfish notwithstanding. It, too, became a target. The brown's ominous mood had every fish in the millrace on guard and afraid to feed.

The old white-haired angler who worked the pool had no way of knowing why his offers were refused. His skills were methodically applied with adroit casts that belied his age, but the frightened trout ignored his efforts.

Puzzled not to catch a single fish, the elder tried changing lures until he exhausted every pattern in his fly wallet. Finally, he took an oversized Muddler from his tattered hat brim. He had put it there to use at the onset of darkness when he knew fish big enough to accept the large fly would start to feed.

A Muddler Minnow fly resembles nothing in particular; it was certainly never tied to resemble a catfish. Its color, however, in the tenebrous water of the Connetquot River after a rain, is precisely that of a mud-catfish. When the large fly drifted down to the testy big trout, he would attack. The great brown would vent all of his fury on the fly resembling the little fish he grew to disdain. He would finally be fooled. He would strike. He would be hooked.

On the first cast up and slightly across the rapid flow from the gristmill, the Muddler sank; its attitude in the current was perfect for the ill-tempered brown. When he saw the lure, the biggest trout ever to live in the river made his move. The ferocious attack of the fish nearly snapped the leader, but the ease of the old angler's experienced hand softened the strike just enough to keep the tippet intact. The #2 hook lodged deeply into the bony jaw, and the fight began.

At first, the fish did not panic. When it felt the hook, it swam immediately for the depths of the pool where it applied a steady force against the resisting line. When it could not realize its freedom, the first issue of fear set into the king of trout.

The fish made a quick run for the rapids and turned its side to the swift current to enhance its bulk against the steady pull at its jaw. The aged fisherman was equal to the task; he gave slack when the fish ran and offered none when it hurried toward him. The old man's skill was severely tested, but he adjusted adroitly to give and take line as the fish altered its fight, pressuring the line with the current and then charging the slack.

The pool was big, but not big enough to spend the length of the fly line, and now a stronger fear coursed through the fish's body and it made another run and a leap. All was futile. The hook held. Now the trout knew real fear. For the first time in its life it felt panic.

The fisherman knew he had hooked a very large fish, but until it jumped he did not realize it was the great brown of his dreams. Brown trout don't usually jump, big ones, hardly ever. So when the great brown took to the air the fisherman panicked, too.

"Why'd you hit my Muddler great trout?" he shouted to none who'd hear. "How'd I fool so large a fish?"

But now that he had done so, his panic was as deeply felt as that of the fish he was fighting. He was terrorized at the thought of losing the great brown of the Millrace Pool. He must win the fight.

The old angler concentrated more acutely on every move the fish made, applying pressure when the fish sulked on the bottom and adjusting when it ran. All was working for the man, nothing for the fish. As minutes passed, the man paid more mind to the time. His worry was that the leader might fray if it continued to contact the razor teeth, but here, too, the man was lucky. The long shank of the big hook held the leader away from the sharp teeth, and the trout had no chance.

Try as it might with flurries of speed, quick twists, strong surges and violent shaking, the great fish could not get free. Slowly, struggle and fear took its toll and the fish began to tire. Gasps for oxygen now preoccupied the fish. The tremendous monarch was humbled and began to give up. Try as it did to keep its equilibrium, the brown's exhaustion began to tilt the fish to its side. This was a sign to the fish and the fisherman that the end was near.

For the fisherman, it could not have come any sooner, He, also, was exhausted. To the fish, dizziness and the need to rest were so overwhelming that its very will for life began to wane. To the fisherman, the sight of the fish turning on its side meant victory, and the love for life waxed within his heart.

To kill so noble a fish was not the man's want, only to catch it. By the time the great brown finally succumbed, floating limply on its side, the old man had waded to a grassy bank to sit and rest. The conquered trout was still in the water at the fisherman's feet. When he extended his shaking, gnarled hand to release the fish, the old man saw the Gray Ghost streamer lodged in the side of the trout's head.

"Oh, so this is why you struck" he whispered as trembling fingers removed the Ghost.

He was about to unhook the Muddler when he looked around the stream to see if anyone witnessed the capture. When he saw no one, he felt the sting of disappointment.

"Who will ever know I caught you great brown? Who would believe an eccentric old man who spent his life in pursuit of a dream?"

For an instant he thought of keeping the fish as a trophy to show what he alone had done. It was an evanescent thought, dismissed as quickly as it had appeared with an urgency to revive the mammoth trout.

After removing the hook, he lovingly supported the gasping trout with one hand and affectionately stroked the grand fish with the other. He gently coaxed water through the fish's gills by holding it upright and rocking it to and fro.

Within a few minutes the trout no longer gasped and the man could feel strength returning to the fish's body. Finally, with a huge sigh and one more glance around the pool, arthritic hands allowed the trout its freedom.

With both palms cradling the vanquished, the old victor gingerly pushed the magnificent fish forward and let it go. With tear filled eyes he watched in amazement as the fish undulated to make a turn back toward him as if to bid farewell. Then the big trout turned again and the old-timer admired the great brown of the Connetquot as it slowly swam towards the depths of the Millrace Pool.

* * *

Late that night the Millrace Pool was quiet again. In its darkest depths lay the great fish – alone. The catfish, now relocated near the pool's shallow tail, beneath a willow overhang, was darting around a smaller mud-catfish, an egg-laden female. They were unaware of the menace slowly rising from the depths behind them, the great brown of the Millrace Pool.

The Double Bibbed Fawn

It was early in the bow season when I first saw the fawn. It was alone, and, I noticed, not cautious like others of its kind. My initial impression was that it was ill or hurt, because the deer let me walk to within 20 yards of it before loping off. The fawn seemed healthy, and despite allowing my intrusion into its space, quite alert. It was one of my most unique encounters in the wild and I could not flush the experience from my mind.

I believed it was a buck. Doe fawns are smarter than that. It's not that they have more brains than a buck fawn; it's because a doe will oust her male offspring long before she pushes away a female fawn. It's nature's plan, not the doe's. Unless some disaster has happened to their mothers, doe fawns are with their parent throughout the winter, getting a longer education than their brothers.

I saw the fawn again a few days later as I made my way towards Oakey Doke, my favorite stand in a grove of white oaks. I knew it was the same deer because of its double bib and the lack of fear it seemed to have of me. We stared at one another for what seemed minutes, though I knew better. In reality, it was more like a few seconds, but for me, a close encounter with a deer seems to linger as I wait for my heart to return to a normal beat.

I wish I could say I'm beyond the point where the sight of a deer in the wild doesn't affect me. I don't panic like I once did, but I wonder what it will take for me to react as though it's as natural as seeing a squirrel. Like the unexpected sight of a friend among strange faces, or the discovery of paired aces as I peek at my down-cards; seeing a deer lifts my cool a few degrees. Though I fancy myself a trophy hunter who passes on immature bucks, even a small doe at a distance is heart lifting. The sight of antlers is heart pounding.

A few weeks later, the rut was just beginning to alter deer activity. I let a sleek eight-point trot past me without raising my bow. I watched him chase a two-year old buck from the vicinity of my stand, circle around and inspect three does sixty yards in front of me. Satisfied that the girls were not ready for his partnership, the amorous buck thrashed into a thicket and disappeared in search of more interested dates. I had just begun to breathe normally when I glimpsed a movement beneath me. Not the least bit phased by the commotion, and oblivious to my presence, strolled the double-bibbed fawn. At twelve feet below Oakey Doke, I got a good look at the young deer and noticed the pride of its gender beginning to protrude through the scalp, confirming my initial thought that it was a buck.

I watched him for a while. He seemed to have sensed my presence as he curiously nosed everything in the area. He playfully pawed the ground, sniffed at the base of my tree and lingered longer than he should have, glancing around as if wondering where I was hiding. Finally, he melted into the thickets beyond the hardwoods, and for me, he became a personification that I named Double Bib.

In the dimming light of the season's last hunt, I was still hoping to fill my tag when I spotted an antler-less deer slowly coming in my direction. On that closing day, venison was my main objective, but I did not want to kill a yearling, especially if it was a buck.

Usually, does are not alone, so I thought it might not be an adult. Without a contrast to other deer, I looked for the longer face and snout to tell me it wasn't a fawn. The animal stopped, turned its head enough for me to see that it had the features of a fully-grown deer. Satisfied that it was not a yearling, I made ready to draw, watching the deer's every movement, waiting for its head to pass behind a branch or brush. At 15 yards away, the deer stopped; its eyes were behind a sapling, my movement concealed. I came to full draw and the deer ambled closer. I sucked in air and held it. Pulse drummed in my ears; I waited for the perfect opportunity.

Perhaps another bow hunter can appreciate the moment when the decision to kill is made. It is that interminable split second right before the touch of the release trigger when thoughts crash together. The ambivalence to take a life collides with the fear of poor execution. The argument between inner voices, one yelling, "wait, wait longer," the other screaming "hurry!" Adrenaline courses through muscles that tighten with anxiety; yet quiver in anticipation. All the practice, all the preparation, all of the skills honed, seem not to help in that instant as my ten-yard pin stutters into the kill zone.

In that microsecond the deer stopped, lifted its hind leg to scratch an ear, and I saw the distinctive, twin, white patches on the throat beneath its chin. I relaxed the bow.

The young buck saw the movement and looked up at me, stomped a hoof several times as if to ask: "What were you thinking?" Then the deer looked away and resumed its trek as though I represented little danger. Elation seemed a strange emotion for the moment, but when I finally exhaled, exhilaration refilled my chest as I watched my breath turn to vapor in the frigidity of December air.

My hunt was over, but not my joy. I thought about that deer for the remainder of the winter and long into the summer. As fall approached, I wondered if I'd see the buck again. I wondered if he would carry significant antlers. I thought about how much he'd grown from when I first saw him to our last encounter, and I supposed he'd be more than just a spike.

I cannot recall another deer preoccupying my mind throughout the off-seasons as much as the fawn. Even those bucks that I chose to pursue over several seasons did not haunt me as much. The only breach to my good feelings whenever that deer would cross my mind was the severity of the winter. With so much snow, and much of it occurring in March, I had my doubts that Double Bib would have survived.

I hunted the first week of the new bow season before seeing a deer. There was no sign of Double Bib and I began to fear the worst. Right before the rut, however, in mid-November, a six-point buck sneaked into my area from downwind. Although I'm in the habit of keeping a vigil looking away form the wind, I would never have seen the deer if it hadn't snorted. The deer was so furtive in its approach that it saw me before I saw it. When it bobbed its head, I noticed that it was Double Bib, and he seemed to be letting me know he was not as naive as he was when he was a fawn. I had no intention of killing the young buck, but I hunted for him each and every time I was in his woods. I saw him no less than a half-dozen times all season, but he always maintained a safe distance from me. It was almost comical to think he wasn't aware of me no matter what stand I chose to use. He'd always glance in my direction as if to show me how much more alert he had become. I knew it was time to hang a new stand.

A few days later as I drove to go hunting, my enthusiasm to get into the woods was at a peak. The area I hunt is not very big, rimmed by residential homes and bordered on one side by a heavily trafficked highway.

As I approached my exit, I noticed several cars on the shoulder of the road. The drivers were out of their cars, apparently examining a deer that had been struck and killed. I pulled over and got out of my Jeep to see the deer. As I neared the scene from behind the animal, I could see it was a buck.

I walked around the deer when I saw it was a six-point. Anxiety grabbed at my stomach as I leaned to look at its neck. When I saw the double white patch beneath its chin I felt the choke of despair grab my breath away. My probe of the deer's teeth told me he was two and a half-years-old, and a churn of nausea overwhelmed me as I sulked away from the scene.

There is no explanation for my reaction. Double Bib was dead and suddenly I lost my desire to go hunting. As I drove towards home I questioned my emotions. In actuality, I had been hunting the young deer all season. But I would not have tried to kill him; I wanted him to live more years.

And, had he become a magnificent trophy, would I have felt differently about killing him? I wrestled with the question, but had no answer because to see him dead, bothered the hell out of me. Again I questioned how I would have felt if I had been the one to take his life, rather than to have him die the way he did. Again I had no answer.

I began to realize that I had more enthusiasm just to watch him and see what he might have become. But why that deer and not the countless others I have taken? Why did Double Bib change my way of thinking? The hunting season was not over; two weeks remained and I had yet to feel the urge to pick up my bow. And I had yet to feel the disappointment for the season's close as I had felt in seasons passed. I wonder if I will look forward to future seasons as much as I have longed for them before I knew of the double bibbed fawn.

The Hole in the Tree Buck

As any serious deer hunter knows, I plagiarized almost all of my title for this story. I owe apologies to one of the most famous bucks of all time for substituting the word "Tree" for "Horn." The pull of temptation overpowered the monitor of my conscience, so I'll suffer the guilt for the subsequent tale.

Before we begin to digest the incredible happenstance of the hole in the tree buck, please allow a little background music. My thirty-year-old son Greg is an unusual deer hunter. Probably very different from most of us who read the wisdom of *Deer & Deer Hunting*. Greg would never pick up any fin and feather related periodical. He'd be more engrossed in *Car and Driver*, more enthusiastic at Lord & Taylor than Gander Mountain, and a lot more comfortable at a desk than in a tree.

Greg would prefer the company of a girlfriend helping him shop for an Armani suit in the coziness of Saks Fifth Avenue, than sitting in a freezing, wind-blown deer stand to bond with his old man. He's a strange person when it comes to hunting, but he loves the first day of the deer season. As long as I buy his license, set out his clothes, prepare his equipment and pack his lunch. Luck is the only ingredient I'm not responsible to supply. Greg brings more good fortune on a hunting trip than a four-lobed clover the size of a palmetto leaf.

The night before the opening of New York's deer season I spent an hour trying to convince him that he should use my 7mm instead of my .270.

"Come on, dad. That cannon's too heavy. Why can't I use the lighter gun?"

"Because the brush is too thick where *I* built *your* stand while you were chasing skirts in Cancun."

"So?" he says with a smile as though he knows I'm jealous.

I had to sneak a quick peek over my shoulder to make sure we were alone. The wife's a mind reader. "So, if you hit a twig or something, the bullet could deflect. The bigger gun will be better in that area."

I'm not so sure he was convinced, but he does have a sense of compassion for his cranky father. "The stand I hunt is a four-hundred-yard walk further into the woods. Uphill!" My moaning about humping the twelve pound 7mm that far must have played on his conscience. I got to use the lighter gun.

There were three of us in our party. My friend, George Johnnidis, Greg and I usually do the first-day honors together. We always use two-way radios when we deer hunt. George and I like to use them – for practical reasons. Greg likes to use them as well; – they keep him amused.

Last to get to my tree stand around sunrise, I finally settled in. The crisp air held enough chill to expose the vapor of my breath, but I knew the morning would yield its cold to the rising sun. It had just begun to peek over the treetops of an eastern ridge, its rays projecting the onset of a pleasant, November day. It seemed like a perfect start to the deer season, and I leaned back against the trunk of the giant sycamore to enjoy the rush of anticipation that the first day of deer hunting had always brought.

An hour later I was startled by a crackling call on the radio. Greg's patience is thinning, I thought. The chatter of hunters on the channels he's been listening in on probably isn't amusing enough.

I took the call. "Yeah, pal," I whisper, "what's up?"

"What's up dad?" he says in a voice as loud as if he were using his cell phone in Grand Central Station.

"You can't be bored already."

"Kinda slow, isn't it?"

"Occupy yourself. Just think about that meatloaf sandwich I put in your day-bag."

"I already ate it."

"Already? What are you going to do for lunch?"

"I thought we were going to go for breakfast in a little while."

I look at my watch. Only 8:AM, time for a little pep talk. "Greg, It's early, but I know we'll see deer. Just be pa...

Booooommmm! I was in mid sentence when the sound of a shot from Greg's direction nearly jolted the radio and me out of the stand.

"What the hell was that?" I yelled. "Greg, was that you? Greg. Greg? Greg, do you copy?"

George answers: "That was Greg!"

"George, he was just talking to me! He had the walkie-talkie in his hand!"

"I know. I heard everything. Well, — he's okay. I can see him from here. He's standing up and looking around."

"That's good," I gasp in relief. "For a second there I thought the boredom really got to him."

As I waited for Greg to make radio contact I was thinking about how lucky he had been on other trips. Some of the most noteworthy hunts are usually those where good fortune is more in abundance than skill. I hate to do it, but I have to be cliché. If you look up "luck" in Funk & Wagnalls: Greg's smile looks back.

I remembered his very first bow-hunt nearly fifteen years before. After hours of making him practice arrow placement, weeks of lecturing about the difficulty of taking a deer with a bow and arrow, we were sneaking into the woods to hang our portable climbers when Greg stumbled over a shed antler.

"I'm going up this tree right here. Maybe this guy will show up," he said brandishing the huge six-pointed antler.

"That was shed last winter," I said trying to persuade him to look for a tree that wouldn't leave him so exposed.

As he fingered the palmated shed, I decided not to dowse his enthusiasm and let him climb a tree that afforded no advantage to ambushing a deer. As he began to climb I stalked off mumbling something to myself about how he took after his mother. I found myself a "better" tree about a hundred yards away and began to climb.

I had no sooner climbed a choice oak and secured my stand when Greg called. "Dad. I got one."

"You what?"

"I got a deer."

I've hunted my whole life and was never more astonished than how he killed that deer. It wasn't the buck that shed the antler, but Greg's first doe had trotted under his stand while he was fiddling around with the shed. He noisily abandoned the antler for his bow, nocked an arrow and drew. All of Greg's commotion stopped that deer ten feet away from his tree.

I have no idea how a mature deer could be so dumb. Mere minutes before, we had to have left enough scent to spook a skunk. Perhaps she was shocked by the ruckus, but the deer stood while Greg took aim at her shoulder. Fortunately, the arrow did not go where Greg aimed for a quartering-away shot, but where it had to go for Greg's luck to make a perfect shot.

Although he never killed another deer with the bow, I think he's backed off the statement he made when I got over to him. "Dad," he said breaking into his signature grin, "I thought you said this was going to be hard to do."

I just scratched my head. "Well, until now, that's what I thought," I said gawking at his skeptical smile as though he had a divine connection.

∗ ∗ ∗

My thoughts were interrupted as Greg finally called. "I shot at a six pointer."

"You what?"

"I shot at a buck."

Normally, I'd have been astonished. Could a deer be so oblivious as to approach a hunter while he's gabbing on a walkie-talkie? Then I reminded myself that it was Greg I was speaking to.

"Is he down?" I asked.

"No. He ran."

"Okay, stay put," I grumbled. "We'll be right there."

As George and I got to Greg, he was standing beneath a poplar sapling looking up at a gaping hole through its trunk. He kept repeating himself. "I can't believe I hit this tree."

"This is kind of a stupid question," I said scratching my head, "but didn't you see it in your scope?"

"I don't remember."

"You don't remember? The tree is big enough to hang a portable stand on," I moaned.

"Which way did he run?" George asked.

Greg pointed north and I kept saying there was no way the deer was hit. We stood under the poplar admiring the fortitude of the tree's ability to stand after being blasted nearly in half by the 7mm. Had he used the lighter gun it would not have done as much damage.

"Was his tail up or down when he ran?" I asked halfheartedly hoping for a good sign.

"I don't know." Greg said, "but he kinda bucked like a bronco."

That got my attention. "He did what?"

"He kicked his hind legs in the air when I shot."

"That sounds like you hit him," I gulped hardly believing my own words. "Let's look around for some sign."

I was never more skeptical of finding a deer, but sure enough, a tuft of hair was proof that Greg's luck was a hell of a lot better than my judgment, and even luckier he used the 7mm. Sixty yards of easy tracking took us to the deer, a two-year-old, very unlucky five-pointer.

When it comes to fortune, that deer's stash of bad luck had to surpass an abundance of Greg's fortuity. For the past two seasons, New York has put restrictions on antlered deer. A legal buck must have at least three points one inch or longer on one side. How Greg saw it is a mystery, or, more testimony to his luck compared to the deer's, but the buck had the misfortune of having an extra tine on his left antler.

For a 180-grain bullet to pass through a tree trunk and have enough of a fragment remaining to do any type of harm seems incredible. But as more testimony to that deer's misfortune, enough of the 7mm bullet stayed intact to cleanly harvest the buck. A better heart-shot could not be accomplished.

No one believes our story when we show the photograph of the tree that Greg's bullet struck before hitting the deer. Who could blame people?

"You should chop that tree down and make a trophy out of it instead of that stupid deer," they said. So, that's exactly what we did.

As far as trophies go, the hole-in-the-tree-buck scored 24 ¾ inches Boone & Crocket. And that was before drying and deductions. Here, I'm too hasty. The deer did have qualification. One, a single inch of antler on his left side making him as minimally eligible as he could possibly be to qualify as a legal buck. But, for George and me, that buck and his one-inch kicker made our day and we headed for breakfast. Along with Greg's enormous smile, we proudly displayed that deer as though he were "The Hole-in-the-Horn Buck."

In Support of Daniel Webster

Does Long Island hold the record for having the largest brook trout to have ever lived? Legend has it that Daniel Webster caught the world's largest brook trout. He was fishing in the Carman's River on Long Island back in 1827 when he landed a 14.5-pound brookie.

Fact has it that the world record brook trout was not caught on Long Island, nor anywhere near New York at all. The record fish, better know as a speckled trout within the environs more suited for the species, was caught in Ontario, nearly a thousand miles away.

Back in 1915, an angler named Dr. J. W. Cook was fishing along the Canadian national transcontinental line, below Virgin Falls when he cast a live minnow into the frigid, swift current of McDonal Rapids on the Nipigon River, and hooked the famous trout. Dr. Cook had witnesses when he landed the 34.5-inch fish that weighed 14.5-pounds, lengthier, but not heavier than old Daniel's fish.

Would the Daniel Webster, who litigated for Jabez Stone against the devil incarnate, Mr. Scratch, create a fish tale? Daniel, too, had witnesses. Mister Carman himself, and half of the congregation of South Haven church (what more credent group?) were alleged to have seen Webster catch a fish that had become legendary to the local gentry.

Many of them had seen the fish lolling in the Carman's River before, and they piqued Mr. Webster's interest. Resolved that he should have the honor, Daniel Webster angled for the huge trout, and hooked it. The slave, Apaius Enos helped land the mammoth trout.

"We hab you now sar!" he supposedly cried out as the fish was boated. The record seems questionable because the Carman's River eventually runs its ten-mile course to the Atlantic Ocean, and therefore likely that Webster's trophy could have been a *salter*, a sea-run brook trout.

Record book brook trout are taken from places like Barbe Lake, in which Tim Matheson of Manitoba caught a brook trout that eclipsed both Cook's and Webster's fish in weight. Because Matheson, a sportsman, released the trout, his world record does not stand, while Webster's trout takes on a stigma of doubt mainly because of where it was caught.

The Carman's River today holds many species of fish, and brook trout can flourish there. In comparison to the Canadian waters that hold monsters, the Carman's River is but a rill. To believe she could yield a world record brook trout is unthinkable to some, but not to me.

Let's not too quickly doubt the angling exploits of Senator Webster, or the capability of where he fished to produce such a record. Another *creek* exists on Long Island that also may prove support for the claim of Daniel, and restore Long Island to its rightful place as home to some of the largest brook trout to inhabit waters anywhere. The Connetquot River in Oakdale, New York is such a stream and has a small stretch of water nearly impossible to fly fish, the only means available.

Many years have passed since I have been there, but the body of water I consider "un-fishable," needs description. It was far up on the back-backwaters of the Connetquot River, near fishing site 24. It may be different now, but then, several hundred feet of river ran there, slow and dark.

As I remember, it was too deep to wade, and unreachable from a fishing platform. The bottomless run was lined on both sides by toothy brush so thick and high making it practically impenetrable. A tangle of wiry growth crawled up from the steep banks like a defending guard-dog and discouraged anglers to even think of attempting the most ill-advised cast. But the collar of growth never put a leash on my imagination for what fish might dwell in the protected pool.

I have walked countless times past that stretch, but never have I not had the insane thought to risk my better judgment, snake my fly rod through the bushes and attempt the unfeasible. Such thoughts were only vainglorious notions that I could succeed to hook a fish, and the idea a fleeting vagary when I considered the possibility of landing it.

Providing I could have burrowed through the gnarly brush, the water immediately beyond appeared deep enough to reach my neck, and a slip into the river from the steep bank would have filled my waders and pulled me under. I'd have had a look at the fishes that dwelled in that sanctuary, but it would most likely have been my final reward before permanently sleeping among them.

I did, however, many times risk scratched skin and a blinded eye to peek through the biting thicket to see if trout were rising in the liquid fortress affectionately named the Black Pool by one of its admirers.

Solitude is the fancy of the angler. To approach a favored stream and find oneself alone is a fisherman's dream, and he would beseech the fishing gods to grant it. But once, when my prayers to find reclusion were answered, I came to the "un-fishable" spot on the gin clear Connetquot and became sorry for heavenly favor. Fighting the brambles, I cleared enough foliage to glimpse through a small opening to see the surface of the pool, and it was then that I saw the largest brook trout I have ever seen. When I caught my breath, about to use it to yell for witness, I did, instead, shout several expletives at my aloneness. Since then, I withhold seeking divine intervention, and subscribe, instead, to the trite admonition of being careful of what I wish for.

I've learned that a rainbow over 18 pounds, and a brown trout about a pound lighter have been taken in the Connetquot. I have seen there a few brown trout I thought nearly as large, but the trout I saw in the "un-fishable" pool was a brook trout, rising and turning just below the surface affording me a look at the white tipped pectoral fins and the orange, blood-red underbelly distinctive of its kind.

Without a witness, I'm not sure if anyone, even Gill Bergen, the State Park's supervisor, believed that I saw a brook trout the size of which I often describe by extending an arm with outstretched fingertips to show how far the trout's tail would reach if its head rested at the middle of my chest. The girth of the fish I saw that day was just as unbelievable, for my first inclination was to think a big striped bass had run upriver from the Great South Bay.

I profess no credentials as an ichthyologist, nor do I boast my skills as an angler. But I've caught my share of trout and consider myself capably familiar with the three dominant species here in the northeastern waters. I know the fish I saw was *Salvelinus Fontinalis,* a brook trout. Perhaps it was a salter that made it from the ocean, or, simply, a fish that lived in a location that afforded it the opportunity to grow to legendary proportions – like the brook trout caught by Daniel Webster in the Carman's River here on Long Island. I think, perhaps, Webster was denied a hearing, a fair inquiry. I would like to be the lawyer in his posthumous trial. "I stand on the Constitution," I'd say as Webster said to Mr. Scratch, "I demand a trial for my client."

The Diabolical Bird

One of the most popular game birds in North America is the pheasant. But the bird's popularity among upland game hunters is somewhat surprising. Though considered a delicacy, as table fare he is not the most delectable choice of poultry. His stringy wings, stubs of sinew built for quick bursts of flight, are hardly worth cooking. His legs, muscular toned for swift running, challenge the chef, and it takes the quintessence of culinary expertise to prepare breast meat with a modicum of juiciness.

Consider that his plumage is most attractive, and that he offers the easiest of airborne targets among game birds, we total his allure. Yet, I was once addicted to the pursuit of the ringneck pheasant, or phasianus colchicus, if the bird's Latin name is preferred. Were it my preference, this marvel of tomfoolery would have several other names, distinguished only by vulgarities.

Seems harsh description for a bird I hold in high regard, but my experiences afield give testimony for expletives deleted. Trust I've used many in trying to outwit the pheasant. He is the embodiment of stealth and incredible evasiveness, the avian master of sneak. His uncanny ability to embarrass the best of bird hunters is difficult to exaggerate, but no hyperbole is too expressive for this old pheasant chaser.

Truth dictates that the pheasant's ability to elude the gunner makes it appear the bird is scarce. Many times the unsuccessful hunter returns from afield to lament the lack of birds. Ironically, could ringnecks converse, it's doubtless untold numbers would return to roost with tales replete how huntsmen crowded the fields making it close to impossible to grab a bite or enjoy a dust bath.

The survival tactics of this Asian alien are so keen as to have us think him a smart bird, when in reality he follows instincts no more cerebral than a dodo's. Though I realize it is not a challenge of mental prowess, the embarrassment

I've suffered in trying my wits against a brain the size of an acorn is difficult to consider. The cock pheasant, despite radiant plumage, is a master of concealment, and regardless of intellect, a commander of patience. And it was perhaps here where my challenge was found for my favorite game.

I have pheasant hunted in many places. I have trampled more paths in the fields of northeastern states than an Appalachian hiker, and I've even tried the famed ringneck haunts of South Dakota. Nowhere, however, have I found the cock-pheasant nearly as abundant or any more challenging than in Quakertown, New Jersey.

Many seasons ago I suffered there a stressful episode that remains evidence to one bird's superiority over this pursuer. The encounter tested my skill as an upland bird hunter and permanently damaged my ego. It began on the first day of Jersey's small game season.

I was taking a friend bird hunting for his first encounter with ringnecks and he depended on my experience to get his first bird. He shall remain nameless, lest his complicity in the incident that decomposed into lawlessness embarrasses him as well as it did me.

On the drive to the farm where we had landowner's permission, my friend became overly excited at a few roadside birds he saw. "Why don't we hunt around here?"

"See those no hunting signs?" I said, "the people around here are serious about trespassers, and they have the whole area patrolled."

His head swirled on shrugged shoulders. "But no one's around."

"Yeah, but fire a few shots and there will be."

"How much farther is our spot?"

"Just up the road about a mile or two, and there are plenty of birds there, too."

We rode for several minutes and admired another ringneck pecking for grit along the road, then drove into a long cindered driveway up to the farmer's barn where he greeted us with a smile.

"Well, boys, there's plenty o' birds around for ya," he said as he handed us our permission slips, "but don't forget, these tags are for my land, and some o' my neighbors don't take kindly to shootin' on their property."

"I know where your boundaries are," I said, "besides, it's hard to miss all those posters."

"Okay, then; you fellas have some fun. See you later when ya drop off the tags."

We thanked the farmer profusely and were off to hunt, certain we'd have some luck.

"Now remember everything I told you," I said to my friend, "and you'll be fine. Just don't let your nerves get the best of you if you jump a rooster. They usually take off with a loud cackle, and sometimes it startles you."

I was full of confidence that my instructions would work as we loaded our shotguns and walked toward a huge cornfield. As we approached the edge of the corn lot the action began. Two birds burst into flight from under my protégé's feet, and a third scurried into the cornfield.

"Hens!" I shouted. "Don't shoot!"

"Damn!" he screamed. "They scared the hell out of me."

"Wait 'till a cock-bird gets up. Then you'll really get scared."

Perhaps I should not have said that because for the rest of the day he took each step in the corn and soybean plots as if they were minefields.

After all my tutelage, my student was expecting to bag his first ringneck. I'd like to say the day was a success, but although I had taken my limit of two birds, I was disappointed for my friend. He had not had my luck, and my promise to teach him how to hunt pheasants went unfulfilled as we turned in our permission slips and headed for home.

The sun was low in the November sky as we drove from the farm and I could not help feeling responsible for my buddy's silence as he gazed out the passenger-side window.

"Stop!" he yelled. "Look at that bird!"

Not more than thirty yards away one of the biggest roosters I'd ever seen strutted boldly amid a field of four-inch-high ryegrass.

"Let's get 'im," he shrieked.

I pulled off the road onto the shoulder and stopped the car …directly beneath a Quakertown poster sign.

"I don't think it's a good idea," I said.

"Oh, man, that's the biggest pheasant I ever seen."

I looked over both shoulders. "I know, but he's on posted land."

"I gotta go home with a pheasant. We can get him from the road."

"No, you can't. He'll take off as soon as you open the door."

"C'mon," he said as he opened the door, "He's asking for it. Let's try."

Instantly, the overgrown bird made a liar out of me. He did not fly, but ducked down in foliage hardly high enough to cover his spurs. He became invisible in the very spot where seconds before he stood flaunting his brilliant plumage and two-foot tail as if he were a flamingo dancing the flamenco.

My protégé was about to get another lesson on the bird's ability to secrete itself in the scantiest of cover. "Where'd he go?"

I felt guilt creeping in. I knew the ringneck would sit tight, squatting in the rye grass and become an easy prize for my friend.

"He's still there," I said looking around to see if the coast was clear. "Get your gun and run over there, but make it fast before someone comes."

"No," he said. "I'll miss him. You do it for me. I really want to bring one home."

Dissertations have no doubt been written on why man goes against his better judgment to become a hero, but I never read one. To this day I cannot say why I chose to grab my 20-guage Browning, chamber three shells and hike for that rooster's harbor in that wide-open field.

I suppose the temerity of that piece of poultry to think it could outsmart me must have ignited my challenge. "Does that idiot bird believe I can't get him?" I yelled as I trotted toward him.

Perhaps the rooster knew more than I thought. He must have felt somewhat less secure as I bore down on him. I had expected he'd burst into flight the moment I kicked at his hiding place under a tuft of cow turf shorter than my boot tops, but he didn't. I could not believe the bird flushed an instant before I got to him and flew — directly at me.

I'd like to suppose there was reason other than poor marksmanship for missing three shots at a pheasant the size of a zeppelin, and nearly as slow. An excuse of surprise that he flew toward me and exactly over my head brought no consolation. The truth was that my volley did not ruffle a single feather, but did disturb the serenity of the pastoral scene.

That evening, more than the tranquility of the bucolic setting became upset. I did not come away from the experience totally well. My equanimity was destroyed as I cursed aloud and watched that feathered freak glide not more than 75 yards across the road into more heavily posted land and alight where I could see him.

Reasoning should have dictated that three quickly fired shots at that particular hour would attract attention. Those shots were most resounding. There was not a single leaf, twig or hint of breeze to muffle the report — nor hinder trajectory, the latter far more disconcerting to my ego.

Common sense escaped. Screaming every swear word I knew, I barreled past my friend, crossed the road and hurdled a low barbwire fence while loading three more shells into my semi-automatic. If the blasts from my shotgun didn't alert the local gentry, the blatant profanities did. But the curses could not mollify my seething temper as they usually would have. Only the death of the demon bird would suffice.

With murderous intent I approached the perimeter of brush into which I had seen the beast of birds go. I shouldered my shotgun and entered slowly expecting a flurry of wings and the bird to explode from cover.

Minutes later, after every twig of brush, stem of grass and wisp of weed was trampled flat, I conceded defeat and allowed that the bird was diabolical. I heaved a sigh, lowered my gun — and nearly succumbed to heart failure as the cock-pheasant blasted form hiding — between my boots.

It will forever be a mystery how I did not see that ringneck. And I may never forgive myself for missing three more shots as he headed for a distant corn lot. But more to my chagrin was the siren of what appeared to be an old police vehicle clanking and thumping up a rutted dirt road in a billow of dust.

Again, I was off and running. Being caught for trespassing was to be avoided at any cost. My figuring was that if a pheasant could escape by going into a cornfield, so could I. In I dived.

The condescending act of crawling on my belly to escape the law was repugnant enough, but my options were limited as I heard the cop on his bullhorn yell: "Come out o' that field and drop your gun!"

His command sounded too serious not to obey, so again I weighed my alternatives. If I surrendered, a sizable fine and a night in jail would have been the least of my troubles; losing the privilege to hunt in Quakertown would have been more than I was willing pay, so I crawled.

I slithered between corn stalks, clambered over pumpkins and gourds wondering why the local police department would own a jalopy. Finally, for what seemed a hundred-yard flight I came to a dirt road at the end of the field. I angled left to stay hidden in the corn and then it happened. My day suddenly became much more interesting than I could have ever imagined. I came nose to beak with the diabolical bird! Neither of us was more surprised than the other.

This time he decided to cackle as he took off. I wasn't sure if his squawk was a result of his being startled, or an attempt to empty my bladder. But the tip-off managed to alert the patrolman, because I could hear the rickety patrol car rumbling closer as I crossed the dirt road on hands and knees and squirmed into the densest brush I could find opposite the cornfield.

I have often wondered how a rabbit could sit tight in cover while a predator stalked perilously close. Would he be frightened? Could he steel his nerves until danger passed? Would he hold his breath to be caught, or expect not to be discovered? Now I don't wonder any more. I acted the rabbit and froze.

Sprawled on my stomach holding my breath, frightened and expecting I'd be caught, I heard the slam of the car door and waited in trembles for the cop to grab me by the nape of my neck and yank me to my feet.

Then I heard him yell: "I know you're in that cornfield, so why don't ya just come on out?"

Before he yelled I thought my continence was in jeopardy, but a sudden calm saved further humiliation as I realized his error. I wasn't in the cornfield as he thought. I was behind him on the other side of the dirt road thanking myself for scrambling across. Able to steel my nerves I listened as he yelled again, but I stayed the rabbit and remained dry.

Once, he was no more than thirty-feet away from me, but shouting into the corn lot. After several more yells, the guy finally gave up. I heard him get into the vehicle and blare out one last time: "If you ever come back here again, I'll get ya!"

The arthritic patrol car creaked down the dirt road until its groans could no longer be heard and I was able to take my first, deep gulp of air. Determined not to move, I waited for darkness to end my ordeal. Several thoughts came to mind as I lay there; most had to do with the old ringneck bird. I was wishing I could have wringed his neck.

I looked up at the sun's dwindling shine as it gilded the tips of the tallest cornstalks; then the rays melted slowly into the horizon behind the corn's yellowing leaves.

"So this is how the end of the day looks to that rooster," I whispered. "Lucky him."

When I thought it was dark enough to move, I slithered from the underbrush and crawled the entire distance of the dirt road until I reached the main thoroughfare and looked for my car. In the distance I could see headlights of cars parked on the road's shoulder and I walked toward them.

The policeman was out of his squad car talking to my friend. As I approached I realized the old man walking toward me wasn't a police officer, but probably a private patrol employed by the farmer's association of Quakertown. "You're the guy who was in the cornfield," he rasped.

I scrunched my brow. "What are you talking about?"

"I saw you taking shots at that cock pheasant."

"Look," I said, "that wasn't me. I got lost."

My friend tried to help. "Yeah, he did get lost. That's why I was drivin' around. I was looking for him when you got here," he said to the guy.

But the geezer wasn't buying it. "You fired at least six shots," he said, his finger inches from my nose. "I saw you!"

There was no way for him to prove I was the culprit, and he knew it, so I decided to smear on more doubt. "You know something," I said with my perkiest smirk, "I'm probably the best pheasant hunter you've ever met. Just look in the trunk and you'll see the birds I got today."

I hated to lie so, but I wanted to get home. "Besides," I continued, "there's no way in Hell I'd ever miss a bird six times."

I took a deep breath, "Do you know that I won the international skeet and trap shooting championship two years in a row?"

The rent-a-cop just stared at me as though he'd never met a world champion skeet shooter and said: "Okay, both of you, get the hell outa here and don't come back."

As we rode home, my silence became too much for my buddy to ignore. "I never knew you won an international trap and skeet championship," he said.

"There's no such contest," I blurted.

"Oh, no? Heck, I really believed you."

Humiliation caught up to me and I felt terrible for lying. I wondered how long it would take for me get over it. But my friend saw me miss the diabolical bird six times, and I have never lived it down.

A Lyon's Last Hunt

The aged lion crouched below the crest of a knoll peering at the horizon; his black mane peppered with gray, rippled in the breeze. Once sulfur embers, his now cloudy eyes were having difficulty focusing on the single file of zebra trotting toward his ambush. As the king of beasts strained against the sun's glare to follow the striped line of equine prey, he moved his regal head for better vantage. A mistake!

The zebra stopped. The lead mare, staring toward the slight movement, neighed softly as her nostrils flared to test the wind, and she did not move. The colt at her flanks, confused now, swung his head around and tremulously peered over his shoulder to see if the lioness, which made the initial charge, was gaining. The young zebra did not realize what its mother had; danger lay not to the rear, but ahead.

The mare whinnied again, turned toward the open expanse of the Serengeti veldt and broke into a gallop with her foal and small herd following to safety. The old male lion lost his purchase. The last chance at a kill the aged lion would ever have escaped with the billowing dust, but he knew nothing of that. He was only a beast with neither scheme nor dream and could not realize the end was near. He would try again, and again he would fail, for he was inextricably bound to the dictates of his nature.

* * *

The old man crouched behind a deadfall and shivered. The winter's frigid bite gnawed into his spine and he fought to control the spasms an icy wind had brought. At an earlier day the hunter could have withstood the discomfort, but now he staggered to his feet to regain circulation. A mistake!

The female deer, only an hour out of her bed was leading her doe fawn to a feeding area when she caught the movement. She stopped, rigid in her tracks, only her ears moved, independently, in the twitching rotation characteristic of her kind. Her nose up, she tested the breeze.

The yearling doe became confused when its mother resumed her trek. The adult doe now veered from her original destination of sweet rye grass beyond the old hunter, turning instead for he security of the willow thickets along a creek bed. When the weathered huntsman glimpsed the flagging tails, he realized his error, watched as the deer ran off, and began to doubt his skills.

Far off on the fleeting deer's back-trail, another deer, an unusually large buck, did not see the man's movement. The huge buck was intent on the doe and her fawn and continued to dog their tracks until finally coming broadside into the old man's view.

* * *

Grenville Lyon loved the great outdoors. His youth knew no greater joy than to hunt the fields and fish the streams, and there he chose to spend his leisure life. His vocation, however, trapped him indoors where for General Motors he made his livelihood in indefatigable loyalty for forty years and got outside only when the whistle blew.

Grenville had another passion: sharing his love of nature. He'd take pleasure in teaching his ken of the great outdoors, and I was his most dutiful student. There is something within the nature of a boy that draws him to the outdoors, the spirit of the wild and its pursuits and so it was for me. Through Grenville Lyon, the lure captured me, and were it not for him who took me afield more than my own father, I would be less today and I owed him for that. The time came to return the gift, repay the debt.

Any man who has ever gone to hunt knows the mind game that exists between concentration and daydreaming. A huntsman realizes that for success, concentration is more essential, though not more necessary. It is nearly impossible to concentrate totally. Concentration is the maturity, the work ethic of the hunt. Daydreaming is the antithesis, the youth, the spirit of the hunt, and as much an integral part of it.

All deer hunters allow fantasy to play into their focus. Such an intervention might be that a magnificent trophy may appear. Gren Lyon had similar fancies for too many years, and nothing is less rewarding in life than to never realize a dream. The burden of eighty-seven years with failing health and dimming eyesight left little hope that the old huntsman would live his dream. I was haunted by that, and wanted to make at least one dream come true for my mentor.

Grenville was a hunter of a small northern state for his entire life. Never having the means to travel to those storied places where trophy deer are taken, he could only dream them. He saw trophy bucks only in magazines, none would ever grace his wall. He would have liked that, but to challenge fate was not his style. His philosophy was simple; he would more likely accept his lot than attempt to change it, but I was not.

I lived close to a huge state park where deer abounded. Many buck deer with trophy-size antlers roam the acreage of those woods, and on occasion become too numerous for the land to hold. Because there is no hunting allowed and no predators exist, the deer must be managed by culling. When overabundance and over-browse threaten the herd, park officials and game management personnel carry out a controlled culling.

Through my acquaintances with the proper authorities, I was able to gain permission for Grenville to be involved with the culling procedure. Because of his age and because he would be harvesting a single deer if he saw one, Gren Lyon was allowed to be the only hunter in the park on a designated day prior to the controlled hunt.

* * *

Six years earlier in late April, the buck was born within a laurel thicket close to a crystalline stream. There he spent his first twelve days before venturing out to follow his mother. Thereafter, his frisky jaunts never returned him to that tangled underbrush. Instead he tagged after his mother wherever the big doe went throughout the remainder of May and into early June.

The days grew in length as did the large fawn's curiosity to roam and he would often venture beyond the call of his mother's bleat. The remainder of his first summer was spent testing her patience with longer journeys away from her guidance. By late August it was obvious the fawn was unique. He was already as big as his mother. His dappled spots had vanished and he was clearly the biggest and most assertive yearling in the park's herd.

Irritating nodules erupted from his head and by late September had burgeoned into bulbous stumps protruding to the tips of his ears. October ended, and so did the doe's tolerance for his testosterone driven overtures. By mid November he became impossible to bear and the growing buck was driven from his mother completely.

The young deer's first winter was difficult, but for his unusual size he survived a severe season of lengthy storms and an early March blizzard that took the lives of all the other fawns.

One full year passed and once again the nodules grew producing thick lengthy beams with three tines on each side. For the next five years the beams and tines of the buck's antlers increased in girth and length until he carried fourteen massive tines, two of which dropped straight down, one beyond each outstretched ear. The deer was handsomely regal and the enormity of his non-typical headgear gave him the distinction of being the largest buck ever to roam the park boundaries.

It was mid-December, half way into the bucks seventh year when the hunt was planned for Gren Lyon. The park was closed, the stage was set and the two old-timers were destined to act out their ultimate roles.

It was late in the day when the enormous buck picked up the scent. Nostrils flaring, he curled his upper lip to draw in more of the pungency stirring his arousal. A doe fawn had come into her first estrous, and it was her scent the buck followed as she trailed her mother toward the rye field of the state park — and Grenville Lyon.

The huge buck, spent from the rigors of the first rut a month before, caught a renewed urge from the scent and loped to its appeal. Far on the back-trail he did not see the movement of the old hunter getting to his feet. Intent instead on the track of the young doe, he lumbered in the direction of her allure and toward Lyon's stand.

Gren Lyon, alerted by its grunts, heard the deer before he saw it. When it came into view he knew immediately the buck of a lifetime was heading to his ambush. At first he tried not to look at the impressive rack. Years of deer hunting taught him that doing so could unnerve a man. He, though, like the buck he was about to kill had been through too many experiences. No mass of bone could best his objective. Now, for the first time in the old hunter's life, dream and concentration converged as he squinted to count the tines of the approaching buck forty yards away.

Try as he could, he had difficulty with the tally. One, two, three tines standing. He thought he could see four, or was it five on the right beam? If the left antler was similar, four standing tines meant a twelve pointer, given the brow tine and the main beam tip.

But when the deer turned toward him more tines seemed to jut from the left side than the right. Could a brow tine be so high? Was that another tine he saw lancing straight downward? He couldn't be sure. Glaucoma was not the obstacle now, tears were. He never finished the count, yet he knew this was the most magnificent whitetail deer he had ever seen.

The dream buck came to a broadside stop thirty paces away. More tears welled as he pushed off the shotgun's safety. Years of deer hunting flashed through his mind. The first buck he had ever taken came to his thoughts. Now his youth, along with that first deer and the many in between were sweet memories. The stately deer before him, though, was something more. It represented every dream he'd ever dreamt, the ultimate fancy come to reality.

Grenville Lyon knew there might not be another return. He knew this could be his final hunt, but unlike the lion, the deer and the other beasts he retained his schemes. Concentration now took control of reverie and slowly the shotgun came up to level on the unsuspecting giant. Once brilliant green, now milky gray, his eyes strained to sight the animal and did finally pierce the misty blur.

His heart pounding, his mind racing, time stood still and Grenville Lyon's finger loosened on the trigger. He held his fire.

Within that millisecond of his lifetime Gren Lyon lost his purchase when the deer resumed its trek. The smiling man was concentrating – to savor the fabulous dream melting into the blear. When it did, it took with it the last chance the old sportsman would ever have.